P. (

Martin Tobin

Vol. 3

SALZWASSER VERLAG

P. Campbell

Martin Tobin

Vol. 3

Reprint of the original, first published in 1864.

1st Edition 2022 | ISBN: 978-3-75259-438-6

Verlag (Publisher): Salzwasser Verlag GmbH, Zeilweg 44, 60439 Frankfurt, Deutschland
Vertretungsberechtigt (Authorized to represent): E. Roepke, Zeilweg 44, 60439 Frankfurt, Deutschland
Druck (Print): Books on Demand GmbH, In de Tarpen 42, 22848 Norderstedt, Deutschland

MARTIN TOBIN

A NOVEL

BY

LADY CAMPBELL

IN THREE VOLUMES

VOL. III

LONDON

M DCCC LXIV

CONTENTS TO VOL. III.

MARTIN TOBIN.

CHAPTER I.

IT'S WELL TO BE OFF WITH AN OLD LOVE, BEFORE YOU ARE ON WITH A NEW.

INSTEAD of leaving Lucy with the Grays, I determined to take her home—so, a few days after our wedding, we began our journey to the lower settlement of the Wanganui, and here we heard of the death of Governor Hobson; he had been plentifully abused during his short administration, and actually harassed to death, having been, it was well known, a delicate and nervous man, when he came out; but although, a few weeks ago, each tongue had been loud against him, I think people were all equally anxious now, to say a word in his praise, dividing, as it were, the private gentleman from the public servant. Mr. Shortland had installed himself as acting governor, much to the disgust of the Wellington settlers. But there being no positive order to provide for such a contingency, of course no one could object, having no remedy at hand, or better authority to quote.

Bad as the prospects of the Wanganuans were during poor Governor Hobson's lifetime, they were, if possible, still more gloomy now, as, in the common course of events, a considerable period must elapse before a new governor could be appointed, and Lieutenant Shortland's feelings towards the company were too well known to admit of any hope of favour or encouragement. Feeling this was no time to think of establishing my claim, or expend my capital in house-building, and as Lucy perfectly agreed with me, we determined to give up the idea of doing more, until a new governor came out, and, meantime, enjoy ourselves in seeing as much as we could, there being little chance of that after we had fairly begun clearing and farming. So, after a short time, spent pleasantly enough at the Wanganui, we took our departure for Wellington, intending to try to find a vessel bound for the north, when I could pay the capital a visit, and, if possible, cross to the Bay of Islands.

Lucy, who had looked pale and ill, seemed all the better for knocking about;

nothing seemed to please her so much as moving; no exposure, or fatigue daunted her. Indeed, after a day's walking, that pretty well tired me, she looked as fresh, and much happier than before, and began immediately laying a plan for another excursion. She would not hear of going to Wellington by sea; so, in spite of the long distance, and hardships to be expected on the unfrequented and wild road that lay between Wellington and the Wanganui—hardships, too, which I had experienced so very lately, I gave in to her wish, and, with a couple of natives to carry our small baggage, we set off upon our pilgrimage.

It would be useless, and, perhaps, tiresome, to go through our journey with us. Adventures, I may say, we had none, except such as served to amuse us at the time, a time, dear reader, when, as you must be aware, very little serves for an adventure, and every little incident has a secret charm. Ah! how fondly and sadly we look back upon such days, long, long years after, How we cling to every treasured incident and prize as priceless memorials every scrap that recalls them. A lifetime almost may have elapsed ; the world and thousands of varied scenes may have passed before our gaze, but once again among the hallowed scenes of the love-lit days memory seems to awake from a long sleep; the intervening lapse of time fades in a dreamy haze, and youth, joy, love, and hope, come back to us like a spiritual presence.

We passed a night at Otaki, where I found poor old Dennis drinking himself to death as fast as he could; the only sober hour he had known, I was told, being one a short time after my departure, when the clergyman visited the station. From Oahau to the Otaki was a short stage, and here we took up our quarters for a few days.

On reaching Wellington, we found the town in a ferment of excitement; the acting governor, contrary to all precedent, having written a long despatch to Colonel Wakefield professing great interest in the Company's settlements, and hinting plainly at a speedy arrangement of the land-claims. The same mail—if such the irregular transmission of letters could be called—had taken despatches to Nelson, authorizing the establishment of a county court, with suitable officers, and promising to keep up at the government expense a constant communication between the different settlements, an advantage, not to mention comfort, little understood within the precincts of a new and young country.

Colonel Wakefield was so much deceived by the deputy governor's protestations, that he determined to go to Auckland and personally represent the wants, plans, and hopes of the Company.

Mr. Johnson had made such good use of my letters of introduction, that I found him installed as a sort of supernumerary secretary to the colonel, and being in possession of private means, and thus able to dispense with a salary, just the man, at that particular period, to get on in the colony. There was already a slight foretaste of the money panic that a few months afterwards paralysed the colony.

I scarcely knew my cottage again, so much had it improved in his hands. New and gay papers covered the whitewashed walls, pretty chintz curtains, chair-cushions, and ottomans had found their way into the sitting-room, together with several little statues and vases, the latter filled with flowers, giving the little room such a bright, home-like air, that I did not wonder when I saw the colour mount to Lucy's face as she thanked him very warmly for his forethought.

"And now, Tobin," said he, after he had seen us into our home, "I'll make my bow. I've got capital lodgings not far off; but take warning, I mean to be a terrible bore, for, upon my word, a lonely life is not the pleasantest in the world; and it was in very desperation I took up the upholstery business. Nay, Mrs. Tobin, you shall not thank me, it was the only chance of happiness I had."

I laughed at his earnestness, and began trying to persuade him to remain our guest, but without effect; and as Lucy did not add her voice, I began to think she did not wish to disturb our *tête-à-tête*, I held my tongue.

No letters had reached me from Slyndhurst, and I began to think every trace of my old passion had disappeared, so more than once I made up my mind to tell Lucy the whole story, but my evil genius whispered why should I distress her with it, or rouse up my own griefs in recalling them? *She* would never hear it from other lips, so why should I disturb her peace? Thus reasoning, I carefully avoided all reference to the Doctor's family when I spoke of Slyndhurst or the past.

The suspension in business which had lately taken place had given the settlers time for a little gaiety, and pic-nics, boating-parties, and even dances became the order of the day.

The club set the example by announcing a ball, which came off in splendid style, the room being quite large enough for the dancers, though too small to admit all the lookers-on, who, as ladies were much in the minority, formed a large portion of the company. There was only one drawback— want of good music—a couple of fiddles, a cornet, and piano doing duty; yet, after all, it was a great triumph for the Wellingtonians to mark down, and, as we heard afterwards, excited no small amount of envy at Auckland.

We also set them an example by our horticultural exhibition, which, considering the age of the colony, was very good, and did us great credit. Most of the old country fruits and flowers were there in great perfection, together with many tropical plants, as well as those indigenous to the soil.

One gentleman had taken great pains and spared neither expense nor trouble to gather all the native products growing in the district, and had succeeded admirably.

Lucy, who was passionately fond of flowers, enjoyed the show more than I had seen her do any amusement.

"You must get me as many of Mr. Clarke's collection as he will spare, Martin," she said that afternoon as we sat in the verandah, Johnson as usual with us, and, as usual, too, we, lords of creation, engaged with tobacco.

"Certainly, darling," I replied; "let us well set to work now. Get a pencil and card, we'll lay out the garden. Nothing like the present moment, Loo, dear."

Lucy produced what was wanted, and proceeded to draw a sketch of a garden.

"I'm afraid that won't answer, Mrs. Tobin," said Johnson, who had risen and was leaning over the back of her chair. "You are throwing all the ground away in walks, and Martin will be down upon you for extravagance. If you will trust me I think I can lay a plan out which will please you. I used to be thought a great hand at landscape gardening; and if you, Martin, will take your wife off to see the foundation of Nelson, I'll promise to have your garden laid out when you come back."

Lucy laughed.

"I shall be eaten if I go to Nelson. Captain Wakefield told me the other day that the natives were the most ferocious in the country. Besides, I should like to see the laying out of my garden much better."

"Then you don't trust my taste?"

"Oh! yes," she replied; "but you know it would be so nice to be proud of my work.

When you are away. you would not care about it, whereas I shall probably be here always."

"That makes me all the more anxious," he said; "it would be a memorial of me."

"There is no necessity. We should not——" she paused, a deep blush mounted to her face. "I mean, I should like to do the garden myself."

"If you mean to fight about the garden," I said, "I've a great mind to forbid it altogether. At any rate, get it settled. I am ready for anything my lady commands. Nelson would be a first-rate trip. Wakefield is always at me to transfer my Wanganui claim there; so, if Lucy takes my advice, she'll let you have the dirty work, and be content with arranging the flowers — eh, Loo? Say the word, and we're off for Nelson."

"By Jove! there's a gun," exclaimed Johnson; "there must be an arrival. I wonder whether it's an English ship. I never heard of any being expected. May I go in for your glass, Mr. Tobin?"

As soon as he was out of hearing Lucy pressed up to my side, whispering—

"Go to Nelson, deary, I was only joking; but don't let him lay out my garden; you shall do that."

As I gave her a hurried promise to see about it, Johnson returned with the telescope, and after a careful survey of the entrance of the harbour, which could be seen from the higher portion of his garden, he called out—

"It's an emigrant ship." "Did you hear of one being expected, Martin?"

"No, not a word. Can you make out her name?"

"No; she's a large vessel, and will be

pretty soon alongside. Come down and have a look at the new birds."

"Will you come, Loo?" but Lucy shook her head.

"I'll be content with your report. I've no friends likely to visit this part of the world."

Johnson and I found the beach crowded. No one seemed to have had any intimation of the arrival, and the bustle and excitement was proportionate. Those only who have been long severed from friends by the wide ocean can have any idea of the interest felt in everything that comes fresh from the old country, and how one longs to see a face that has come straight from home.

Letters are priceless in their way, but how much more precious the eyes that have looked upon the treasured scenes, and lips that can describe them as they now are. I have often envied my fellow colonists their home interests, and wondered how I should feel if I met some old familiar Slyndhurst face. And even now, as I stood on the deck of the "Fife," the thought was strong in my heart, and tears actually sprang to my eyes as I watched a reunion of some old neighbours, and heard the often repeated words, "What is so and so doing? God bless him."

"Here he is, Miny, by all that's glorious," shouted a cheery and well-remembered voice at my elbow.

My very heart ceased beating, the ship seemed reeling under foot, as turning I looked into Dr. Millard's face, and beyond him saw another absolutely radiant with joy, springing past her father, and forgetting everything except that she saw me again, Miny threw herself into my arms.

For a second or two I was as a man in a dream.

"You are ill, poor boy," said the doctor, half supporting me on one side, while Miny, now pale and frightened, still clung to the other arm.

"We had no notion of it, poor fellow! You should have written. Even Miny began to think you had forgotten her, poor fellow! I must take to my old trade again, though I fancied doctoring was a dead letter in these parts. Come down to the cabin, my boy! You want quiet."

Mechanically I followed him down, and drank half a tumbler of brandy and water.

Johnson had never left me, and now came forward. The tone of his voice, and the expression on his face brought me to my senses. I never saw horror, indignation, and despair so plainly blended in a face before or since. It told me all, although I only saw him for a moment, and when I looked up again he was gone.

"You feel better now, do you not, Martin?" asked the doctor, anxiously, his hand on my wrist."

"Oh! yes——yes. I cannot tell what upset me."

"Why you look strong enough, certainly, but, I suppose it came so suddenly; but it's your own fault, you never gave us your address; so how could we write? But after the letter you wrote about poor Frank, Miny chose to take on in such an absurd way. So after frightening me out of my life, I sold my practice, and came out to seek you. Strange enough to hit upon the very spot.

"Strange, indeed," I muttered, not knowing

what I said. Then there was a silence, interrupted by the doctor saying—

"Miny, go to your sister. Martin and I will go on shore; you had better stay in your cabin, I'll find out all you require, and you'd best get all your information from me.

"Nay—no love scenes, Miny," he said, harshly, "off with you, he and I will settle everything."

With a merry laugh in her eyes, Miny gave a look and obeyed her father, who as soon as she was out of sight, turned on me, and laid his hand heavily on my shoulder. He had seen and read my agitation too well.

"What is it, Martin Tobin? Have you played her false? Are you married?"

"I am," I said, my lips growing cold and

stiff, as if my death-sentence had escaped from them.

"Then God forgive you for a heartless blackguard, and pity my poor child!"

CHAPTER II.

THE FIRST STEP UPON A SAD PATH.

"You might have waited a little longer for an answer, Martin," observed the doctor, when I had told him all; "my poor girl deserved it."

All the answer I could make was, to cover my face, and groan. I seemed to have forgotten Lucy, with all her love and gentleness; and even then almost involuntarily I blamed her as the cause of my misery—for such I deemed it.

"Why had she married me? She knew

I had loved another; she told me so herself. What matter if I denied it? She ought to have known better.

How long I sat brooding weakly and madly overy my fate I know not. I was roused by a light hand resting on my head, and Miny's own dear voice addressing me by name, bidding me look up and listen to her. With a shudder lest I should see some terrible change in her face, I raised my eyes, hard and burning with unshed tears.

"Miny! Miny! can you forgive me?" I gasped, hardly knowing what I said.

"My poor Martin!" she said, kneeling down beside me, "God help you and me too, for there is no use trying to hide that I came here to seek you. But I do forgive and pity you from my soul. I'm not going to think of myself, Martin; I am thinking of you. You are worse off than I am. You must let me see your wife, Martin; if she loves you, I shall be happy. Nay, dear! don't cry. Indeed! Indeed! dear, I cannot bear it, unless I know you are happy, and that you are doing your duty. My father has told me, and I will love your wife if you will let me."

By some struggle I checked my tears, though the effort made my brain whirl.

Then she rose, sitting down by me she took my hand, and held it firmly as she said,

"Martin, if you loved me as truly as I loved you, you will listen quietly, judge for yourself after I have spoken, but do not be hasty. You will think I am heartless and cold, perhaps. I have had time, and am comparatively alone. You *must* let me see your wife, Martin; she shall be my sister."

"And you, Miny, you?"

"Trust me, Martin, I shall love her; I said so before; did you not hear me?"

"Yes."

"You did not believe me then. But you are wrong, Martin. I can understand it all, and pity you from my soul; but I pity her more, Martin, indeed I do. I am a woman, and know what she would feel, if she knew, but she must not. You must not tell her, Martin; if you do, I must go away. I could not stay then."

As a drowning man is said to catch at a straw, so I caught at the hope. It was like a reprieve, and one had I thought of, I should have deemed too wild to propose.

"I consulted with papa, Martin, and he agrees with me, that unless you told your wife before of your—, of me, I mean, that it would be kinder to her, and better for you, not to do so now. She would think you had deceived her;—do not think I am cruel, dear. I must either be as your sister or go away altogether. There can be nothing else for us. Papa thinks we should not stay, but—but—"

Poor Miny! she had spoken very quietly until now. Now she covered her face, and turned away, trying to regain her calmness. It was my turn to comfort her. Her strength had carried me with her through the first burst of anguish, and such being my nature, I seemed to have buried the pain. The surprise was over. Thought and reason had come to my aid. The events of the past months had risen before me, not in judgment as they had often hitherto done, but as kind witnesses to exonerate me from the guilt I had at the first outburst laid to my charge.

Although Miny had said nothing of this, I felt she penetrated my thoughts, but as I grew strong she grew weak. She had truly thought of me before to the utter exclusion of herself. Now she had made me victor she had nothing to tear her thoughts away from her own misery.

"It cannot be, Miny," I said, sadly. "You know not what you ask. I have not wronged you intentionally, and have done no wrong to my poor wife that she will not forgive me when I tell her. I must do it, Miny."

"You forget me!" she exclaimed, starting up, and looking at me, her eye flashing through her tears—"you forget that I can feel. Do you think I am going to stay to be pitied by *your* wife—to be pointed out as—"

"Miny! Miny! why will you try to

break my heart? You may know some day the trial you are putting me through now, and you will thank me."

"Never, Martin. If you tell your wife, I shall not stay—I cannot. Do not send us away. My father is dear and kind, but since mamma died he has not been the same. And oh! Martin, I'm alone. I often want advice. You don't know what I mean, and I'm almost ashamed to tell you. Papa had lost a great deal of his practice, or would not have sold it. Mamma's influence had kept him steady, Martin, but I cannot."

She hid her face, and sobbed bitterly.

Truly my temptation was strong, coming too from the pure lips of one I would have given my life to save from a moment's uneasiness, much less pain. I knew too well the wretched life Miny might anticipate if her father continued to give way to the vice of drunkenness, one too prevalent in all young colonies, and only kept under by the constant necessity for action, and continually pressing wants of the day. It is too well known that a man with a small independence, and the latent inclination to indulge in stimulants, is almost sure to become a hopeless drunkard in a colony. Poor Miny! Could I send her away? or, as bad, leave her, to meet all this alone, and worse, with her three little motherless sisters all looking to her for counsel and help?

Presently she looked up; then, rising, held out her hand.

"Good-bye, Martin. I see it cannot be. Perhaps you are right. I am only a girl, and know so little beyond home.

I should like you to advise papa where to go, if you would not mind."

"My dear, dear Miny! do not speak that way. I'll do anything you wish. God help us both. I thought as much for you as myself; but you may be right; God grant it! Poor Lucy!" I murmured, half unconsciously, and with a heavy pain at my heart, a sort of presentiment of the evil that was to come so soon, so soon.

I saw Miny's cheek grow pale, and a convulsive movement in her lip, but she did not speak.

"Go away, now, Martin," she said, glancing at the timepiece and shuddering; "I shall tell papa. You can bring *her* to see us to-morrow; she cannot object to your old friends being near."

Miny spoke the last sentence almost bitterly, and as Lucy's trusting, loving face came before me it grated harshly on my ears.

When I reached home I found Johnson alone with Lucy. She looked pale and weary, and an expression of intense relief flushed her face as I entered.

"Oh! I'm so glad you are home, Martin! I could not persuade Mr. Johnson to go away till he saw you safe. I began to think you must be in some terrible danger.

"So I was, Loo, love," I said, "in danger from bright eyes and meeting old friends again."

Something in Johnson's expression of face prompted me to say this. He must have seen it, I think, for he turned away with a sneer, and interrupted Lucy before her exclamation of interest could be spoken.

"It must be charming to meet old friends

in a place like this. It made me quite envious; but I shall leave him in your hands, Mrs. Tobin; only if I were a wife I should keep a sharp look-out upon such old friends."

Lucy laughed gaily, and scarcely deigned to let him out of the room before she had put her arms round my neck, and nestled her sweet face up to mine.

"Come, pet! tell me all about them. He has been trying to make me jealous, telling me all sorts of things. Do you know, Martin, I've a secret to tell you. You won't be vexed with me, or ashamed of me?"

What could I say or do, but kiss the bright eyes, and try to laugh at her eagerness?

"Well, dear, before you asked me to be the proudest, happiest little woman in the world, I fancied—mind, I know now it was only fancy, not real love a bit—that I cared for Mr. Johnson."

It was well she hid her face, for mine must have grown livid.

"You are not angry, darling?" she said, looking up after waiting for me to speak. "Oh! Martin, dear, dear husband! what have I said? what have I done?" and she clung shivering to me with love and fear in her eyes.

"Nothing, pet," I gasped. "I'm not very well, I suppose. But it is so strange; it seems almost supernatural. I will tell you afterwards; tell *me* now. What made you say this about Johnson to-night?"

"Because I dislike him so much; and he looked so—so—. Oh! I don't know, dear. But when he began telling me you had met an old friend, and describing how pretty she was, and how glad to see you, and so surprised when you said you were married, I hated him. I think I must have let him see it, though I tried not, in case of displeasing you. I thought I would tell you first, dear; and that if he knew how I hated him he might do something to make us unhappy. You know wicked people can do so much, and I know now he is wicked."

Lucy held me so tight in her arms that I could not see her face. I knew from her voice it was pale and indignant. I could not speak; my breath seemed choking me, my brain was whirling, while remorse and shame made me shrink from her embrace.

"Come to the light, Martin," she whispered, untwining her arms, and leading me towards the table. Then taking my hands in hers, she stood before me gazing stedfastly in my face, her own pale at one moment, but flushing and working nervously the next. "Are you angry, dear?"

"No, no, darling, my own true wife, a thousand million times no!" and laying my hand upon her shoulder, I tried to check my sobs, for believe me, reader, men can cry; and though tears are wrung forth like drops of blood, they bring relief to the heart, and ease the burdened brain as nothing else ever can or will do.

Lucy grew frightened, and I suppose not knowing what else to do, began to ask me to forgive her.

"Darling, do not be angry, do not be sorry; I never loved him—I only thought I did before I knew what love was. Oh! my pet, my own dear husband, you cannot doubt my love to you. Nothing but death can part us in this world, and that will only unite us for eternity. I did not mean to say anything of your friends, dear—I'm thankful they've come. I knew I was not your first love, Martin, although you were so kind in trying to persuade me I was. I knew you had been engaged to some one in England, and that she had been unkind to you. Dick Hyde told my sister all about it, and that he knew the girl, too. I wanted you to tell me yourself, dear; I knew some day you would, and always watched for it when you spoke of old times. Has she come, darling?"

"Dear Lucy! true wife! your dear lips were on my cheek when you breathed rather than asked the question, which, but for your truth, might have raised a dark, impenetrable wall between us for ever. As it was, I felt a weight lifted from my heart, and looking into her eyes, I said—

"Yes, Lucy, dear wife, she has come"—a deep flush and quick dilation of the blue eyes was all the change. Then she drew me closer and whispered—

"Tell me more, beloved; did she forsake you, or—oh! surely not! Have I come between you?"

"It is a long story, darling; the old, old story of mistake and mistrust, though it now seems all on my side. Do you know, Lucy, she came here to seek me and tell me so."

Then I told her all,—everything Miny had said, everything I thought, hoped, or feared. I laid my heart open before her, as open as it lay in the sight of the great Judge. When I had done, and my confession was made, Lucy looked into my face with a clear, tearless smile.

"We shall still be happy, Martin; we have no secrets now, and, please God, never will have. You will take me to Miny to-morrow—she shall be our sister. She will, I hope, forgive me, and, some time, learn to love me. I did not mean to make her unhappy, you know, and neither did you, dear."

Next morning Lucy could not rest until I consented to take her to the boarding-house to which Miny and her father had gone.

"You had much better let me tell her I know all about it at once," she said. "Depend upon it I am right. I know what she must feel, and your comfort would only aggravate her pain."

And so I was fain to let things rest in her

hands, convinced that whatever she did it would at least be for the best.

I never heard exactly what passed during that morning, and what I did hear is to me too sacred to repeat.

Lucy was sitting with Miny's hand in hers when I entered the room. Both had evidently been weeping, and Miny's face had an expression on it perfectly new to it: one, I felt, ought not to be there, and which chilled and left an indelible expression upon my mind.

"I shall leave you to tell your husband our plans," she said, rising hurriedly; "I must tell papa."

"It is all right, my poor boy," whispered Lucy after the door closed; "poor fellow! I am very sorry I came in the way. She's a dear girl—far better than I am. She's just like my poor sister, Martin, and I love her already. She told me about her father—isn't it dreadful? Now we must try to make up to her in other ways the misery we have caused her."

CHAPTER IV.

THE FIRST SHOT.

"HAVE you any commands to the metropolis, Martin?" said Johnson next day. "I am off in an hour, and mean to ask the new Governor when he comes out to make me 'warden of the woods and forests.' If he's as great a fool as he's likely to be, he'll do it, no doubt."

"Are you really in earnest, Mr. Johnson?" exclaimed Lucy, very much surprised, and I verily believe with true feminine vanity, just a little offended that he should speak so carelessly of leaving her presence, though, on the whole, I knew his absence was as much desired by her as by myself. For, in spite of all, I could not feel the same towards him as I did before Lucy's confession, and the suspicions that it had engendered in my mind. I did not believe in him, and was heartily glad when he was gone.

The settlers being so terribly healthy that, saving a stray accident or the happy enlargement of a family, a doctor's profession became almost a dead letter. There is nothing like novelty, however, and for a while Dr. Millard had plenty of patients, and made a very good thing of it. Miny was too busy arranging and working in the house to see much of either my wife or myself; and though Lucy never let a day pass by without paying her a visit and helping in any way she was allowed to do, I saw Miny avoided her with a sort of cold civility. Poor Lucy tried for a long time to shut her eyes to it, and never spoke to me of it, until I remarked how changed Miny was. Then, with many tears and self-reproaches, my gentle wife confessed how much she had tried to be her friend, but never made a step further; rather, indeed, retrograding.

Wellington was now a thriving and populous little place. Balls and parties of various kinds came off frequently, and the sporting fraternity were deep in the mystery of book-making for the proposed races, to be held as soon as Colonel Wakefield returned from the north. Johnson had only absented himself for a few days, and, professing to have changed his mind, and a determination not to move until he had heard from England, had again taken up his old quarters; and though nothing had passed verbally, we seemed to understand each other better: he did *not* make our house his home now, but having made great friends with the doctor, danced attendance upon Miny whenever she appeared in public.

A month or two passed away, during which I began speculating in various small ways: Hinon bark dye, some of the finest sorts of woods applicable for ornamental furniture, and lastly bundles of flax cleaned as well as the natives could manage it; these I sent home as experimental stock, and waited the result.

We had been very gay too, and Lucy seemed to have taken up altogether a new plan, going to all sorts of parties, and insisting upon chaperoning Miny whenever she could persuade her to accompany her, a proceeding which did not quite suit me, as I found that somehow something of the true state of things that led to the intimacy had become known. People were just then idle enough to like to talk scandal, and though they had abundance to comment upon, they all seemed to set their wits to work to discover the secrets of my poor little household. Lucy knew nothing of this, though I am sure Miny did, for she began to avoid people, and over and over again refused going into society, alleging that she had enough to do to keep her busy at home. And truly I began to see she had; for though her father's patients increased rather than diminished, he had to draw largely on his private income, and began to dabble in all sorts of wild speculations, listening to every Sydney adventurer whom he fell in with, and turning a deaf ear to any warning voice. But worse than all, his old vice began to get the upper hand.

Poor Miny was absolutely powerless. Her affection had at first strongly operated in keeping him sober, but gradually that, too, lost power. I tried all I could, but equally in vain; and unless some great turn in his fortune or affairs took up his attention, I saw nothing but wretchedness before him.

New Zealand was at that time a rendezvous for men of all countries and all characters, many of the worst being from England. And as a proof how much upon the guard the old and respectable settlers thought it prudent to be, they would not admit any new member to the club until he had not only been proposed and seconded by two vouchers, but his name had been posted for six months, and thus open to any examination and inquiry. I had at the outset got the doctor nominated in the hope of keeping him out of another club, formed by those who knew they had no chance to be admitted to the first, or had actually been refused; and it was with no small amount of vexation I found he had actually joined them, alleging he could not wait six months for the ballot.

Upon Colonel Wakefield's return from Auckland he raised our hopes by the information that acting Governor Shortland with his wife and suite were actually then *en route* for Wellington, the government with the best intentions, he asserted, wishing to settle all the long postponed land disputes. Great was the rejoicing; preparations for a suitable reception were at once commenced; the races were put off to be honoured by his presence; the bachelors sent out invitations for a ball, on a scale of magnificence hitherto unattempted; the upper club talked of a banquet; innumerable private *fêtes*, picnics, and balls were planned and agreed upon.

Indeed, it seemed that the good folks of Wellington were determined to prove their prosperity to the Governor, and make up for their want of hospitality to poor Governor Hobson. Lucy, having become quite a leader among the fashionable people, was to preside as lady-patroness of the bachelors' ball, so thought it a favourable opportunity to give one herself.

Accordingly I was deputed to collect materials, &c. for a hut, which I was nothing loath to do, enjoying a bit of gaiety as much as any one, and none the less either that it amused and pleased my dear wife, who seemed to win the admiration and affection of every one, from her gentle kindness and readiness to do anything to forward their amusement, not forgetting good and earnest advice when she thought it necessary.

When Lieutenant Shortland arrived, he

must have been not only gratified, but surprised at the trouble taken to insure this visit being a pleasant one. And though he did not by any means act so openly and fairly about the land-claims as we expected, and as he might have done, if left to judge for himself, we relaxed nothing in our bill of fare, and I heard afterward that he had said "he would rather be ruled in Wellington than rule at Auckland." Mrs. Shortland pleased every one, and carried many a good wish away with her.

One effect of the gaiety was to keep Dr. Millard sober. He had known some of the Shortland family in England, and had concocted a plan which he kept to himself, even from Miny, until he had gained his point, and that was to get a promise from the acting Governor to give him the first medical charge in his power, and use his influence with whomsoever might succeed him as governor. Meantime he was to have a grant of land at Auckland, and any stray work the government could give.

As I said before, I knew nothing of this plan, although Miny would not believe me, and openly accused me of having done it all. It was no use denying it, no use pointing out the advantage therein held out to her father, and the prospect of such good fortune; she would hear nothing, asserting passionately it was either my doing or my wife's, adding she knew Lucy was jealous of her, and could not bear to see her.

I had patiently enough listened to her blame of myself, and even of Lucy, until she spoke of jealousy. Then I felt I had no right to hear more. I had watched my wife ten thousand times, and felt persuaded I perfectly understood every action and thought. With a faith and love far surpassing all I had any conception of, and for which I could never sufficiently prove my gratitude, she had never questioned or attempted to control me. She had tried to be a sister to one she knew *I* had loved and might still love. She had never suffered a cloud to darken our home, or a single allusion to the painful subject to enter into the present peace; and, reader, need I say she had taken a place in my heart far higher and deeper than Miny ever had, or, I now felt, ever could have done. Next to heaven itself Lucy was all in all to me; and when I now look back, after long years, she seems to me to have been fitter for heaven than earth; for who but an angel could have saved me then from the worst enemy man ever has, his own evil passions.

Even Miny, dear as she had been, had gone too far. Her words stung me to the heart, and wisely, or unwisely, who can tell which? I told her what I felt, reminding her of my first advice.

"Then you think I am trying to win back your love, Martin," she exclaimed, angrily. "Do you wish to drive me mad? Have I not had shame enough? Have I not had as much to bear as she has? Look at her, now look at me? Who is changed most? Truly enough she has the right to love you, I have not. And yet, and yet—time will prove whose love was purest. I may never see you again; indeed, after what you have said to-night, I will not do so. But let me say one thing, you love *her* above all the world now, and she loves you; do not let her ever have cause to doubt you with another. Be open and true, or you will bring shame and misery not only on her but yourself; and if her, then upon me too. I cannot tell you all I mean or fear. I hardly know what it is myself. I might have saved you something if we had been here; but now I must only pray for you. Remember my last words, Martin, perhaps my last on earth,—never give her cause to be jealous, or you will make earth a hell for you both."

I saw Miny was angry, and paid little heed to her incoherent words, leaving the house soon afterwards.

"You never told me, Miny and her sisters were going with the Governor's wife," cried Lucy, running into my room the next day. "I have just seen her, and bid her good-bye. She said she told you last night, and did not wish to speak to you again. Why you idle deceitful boy, you must have a secret penchant for her yet, or you would have told me all about it. Why did she keep it so quiet?"

"Her father only told her a couple of days ago, I believe," I replied, carelessly. "Poor Miny, she is better away. You'll think me a conceited fool, I dare say, little woman; but I am afraid Miny was not getting on so happily as she ought to be."

Lucy's face grew grave.

"You are right, dear. I cannot help telling you, but I do not think Miny has been behaving quite as she should do. She forgot that you had no right to love her, and that I was very forbearing to do all I did. Indeed, Martin, I don't want to praise myself; but sometimes I felt as if I could not go on laughing and being merry, when I did not feel sure whether you might not still love her best. It was a hard battle, dearest. They talk of a soldier fighting, and charging in a battle. But I think there's many a bloodless battle fought in the homes of everyday men and women, which would not shame the proudest victory on record. They talk of the weak nature of woman, of their frailty, and all that; but I'm sure many a woman goes through trials in the secret of her own heart that, that——"

And here dear Lucy having worked herself into a flood of tears began to sob, and cling to me.

I could pet and comfort her by telling how much better I loved her now than ever I thought I could do, even when I thought I loved her most, how disappointed I too had been with Miny, and how relieved I was to think they were going so far away. So my dear little wife dried her tears.

I did see Miny again in spite of her assertion that I should not; the doctor left his affairs, speculations and what not entirely in my hands to wind up, continue, or do as I thought best with, and insisted upon my accompanying them on board the government frigate to drink success to his voyage and new appointment.

When they were gone Lucy grew dearer than ever; and soon another happiness came, namely, the prospect of seeing a small counterpart of my dear wife; a prospect which, though its forerunning troubles paled her cheek, and brought a strange look of suffering in her face, gave a deep light to her eyes, and a new force and depth to her love.

The affairs of the Company had been a little more lively since the visit of Mr. Shortland. Nelson was progressing steadily, several hundred well-to-do and promising emigrants had gone direct to the settlements, and were clearing largely all round the bay; while a very fertile valley, called Wairoa, had been partly surveyed, the party however being stopped by Raupahara, of fighting renown; upon which Captain Wakefield, a brother of the Colonel's, and director, &c. of the Nelson colonists, thought it better to wait a little, and refer the claims and rights to the land court.

When Colonel Wakefield heard of the interference of the great Maori warrior, he at once called a meeting, and took the advice of the majority as to the best mode of dealing with Raupahara in case he carried his arrogance to any higher pitch, it being very well known that he secretly paid and encouraged the natives, who were, inch by inch, disputing the Hutt valley with the settlers.

I think the generality of the settlers very much underrated Raupahara's abilities and qualities, which from all I saw and heard were of the highest order both as general and diplomatist. From the outset he had opposed the system of colonization, while he welcomed the colonists, to whom he would have willingly sold land, and he naturally enough objected to another governor stepping in and taking the reins out of his hand. This we can scarcely wonder at, considering his position and birth, as also that he was partly educated. He had hitherto been very careful to keep at peace with the settlers, and had never come so near a rupture before, so now it behoved us to be on our guard.

On my return from this meeting I found a message waiting from my friend Richard England, who had been speculating for me in building. He had held out such an encouraging prospect of the way things were going on, and the investments open to any one with a little ready money, that after consulting with Lucy I made up my mind to go over to

Nelson the first opportunity, which happened to be the following week.

Johnson offered to accompany me, but at the last moment found he was required at the Colonel's office; and with great seeming regret gave up his expedition. I did not feel very sorry, for, as I said before, our old intimacy had been considerably broken, and we now seldom saw him except in an ordinary visiting way.

Nelson had truly made marvellous steps in the march of civilization. Streets were marked out, and, in many cases, in process of building. Two large warehouses stood at a convenient distance from the proposed dock. Captain Wakefield's pretty cottage looked a perfect bower, so environed was it with shrubs and creepers. Already the prosperity since attained by this favoured town was in the bud. Nor was it difficult to account for this. The pioneers of the settlement were all picked emigrants, scarcely any of whom had left England without a small store of ready money; and those few who had come out passage free to seek a fortune had brought with them first-class characters, and what is in truth *the* best fortune for a colonist, willing, hopeful, and honest hearts. Merry faces and cheerful voices greeted one on every side, and the healthy rosy cheeks of the children, some of whom I had seen on board ship at Wellington tottering about with white faces and red swollen eyes, spoke volumes for the invigorating climate. My friend put me into what he called his best room, which consisted of an outhouse, half of it occupied by a fine young thorough-bred he lately had imported from the old country, and for which two hundred pounds was considered a low figure when I bought him some days after, half in memory of my poor friend, half in admiration of the horse himself.

I now heard the true version of the impudence of Rauparaha, and heartily acquiesced in England's opinion, that he ought to be well blown up by the government, and the survey insisted upon, not only for the sake of the safety of the settlers at Nelson, but of the peace of the colony; as, if the natives once got an idea that we were afraid of them, there would be an end to all hopes of peace or established colonization. Besides, at this juncture, it was most desirable that the settlers should be permitted to show their determination and strength.

Lieutenant Shortland had failed in his wish to punish some natives on the Thames, who had committed several outrages, and who (when the acting governor was dissuaded by some of his friends and the missionaries from taking the matter into his own hands, and punishing them as they deserved,) openly laughed at the threats they had heard, and gave out that the English were afraid to fight them; and thus, I believe, was laid the first stone of the structure of trouble and mistakes that has since become visible to the whole world, the harvest of which is even now (when this is passing the press), being gathered with sickles red with colonial blood.

The day after my arrival the surveying party again made an attempt; and this time not only were they stopped, but their huts burnt to the ground by Rauparaha's followers.

The excitement which now prevailed in Nelson was painful. Timid people were loud in their prophecy of evil, and were already preparing to cross the straits. Many others waited upon Captain Wakefield, urging him to assert the authority of the law to which Rauparaha, as a subject of the Queen, was amenable, and arrest him for burning the huts.

Unfortunately, as events turned out, Captain Wakefield allowed himself to be overruled, and, I believe, contrary to the dictates of his own more prudent, though none the less courageous, nature, consented to go with a party of magistrates and constables to arrest Rauparaha.

The event is too well known: a hasty word, a hasty chat, and the passion of the natives burst all bounds. They overwhelmed the handful of Englishmen, took half of them prisoners, and then mercilessly butchered them in cold blood. And when evening fell upon the lately smiling and joyful little settlement, with it fell the gloom of death and murder. For such, let Rauparaha and his friends extenuate it as they will, was the massacre of the Wairoa.

CHAPTER V.

THE ENGLISHMAN IN DISGUISE.

It had been frequently suggested that the natives obtained assistance from fugitive convicts; and that men who, escaped from penal servitude, took refuge in the disguise of tattooing and fraternising with the natiyes, were the most implacable and bloodthirsty enemies the colonists had to contend with. The fact of some of these men having been soldiers, may account for the strategic operations adopted by the Maories. Many attempts had been made by the settlers to obtain further information on this head, especially in regard to one man, who, although under a Maori name, and adopting every characteristic of the natives, was well known to be an Englishman, and not a common one either, as evinced, not only by the advice he gave to Rauparaha, but by several letters to other chiefs which, from time to time, had fallen into the hands of interpreters and others, and which plainly showed a man of education and talent.

Many romantic stories were told of his deeds of daring and adventure, since his appearance in New Zealand, most of them agreeing to prove one point, namely, that he had been a soldier, that he was intimately acquainted with military work, and possessed the power of ordering and disciplining others, as was evident from the way in which the natives had learnt several difficult manœuvres, not to mention their clever defences, and attempts at fortification.

One of the unfortunate fellows who had accompanied the Wairoa party was convinced he had not only seen this man, or Kauri, as he was called on account of his great strength, but fought him single-handed, and in true British fashion, namely, with no other weapons than nature had bestowed, and which no one but an Englishman knows how to make proper use of. Kauri, it seemed, not only knew how to use them, but did so scientifically, this, my friend told me, was certain. Rauparaha had at first come in for the full measure of hatred, but now his name was almost forgotten beside that of Kauri. Curses both loud and deep were heaped on his head; a few of the colonists going so far as to bind themselves with an oath, to bring such a wretch to justice.

After the affair at the plains Rauparaha retired hastily and by night to the neighbourhood of the Marrawatu river, taking up a position of considerable strength at Otaki, in a pah already fortified by outworks; and it was reported, containing a much larger stock of arms and ammunition than could have been in the possession of the natives unless secretly supplied by traders, who had frequently been suspected of bringing out muskets and ammunition in exchange for Kauri gum, &c.; and as Raupahara had emissaries at all the ports, he could easily obtain what he wanted in this way.

As soon as the accounts of the Wairoa affair became known, outlying stationists began to flock in, rather incurring any loss of property than the risk of being butchered by the natives.

A general, but scarcely to be wondered at, panic soon prevailed, and before I left Nelson, which I did as early as possible, a meeting had assembled, and drawn up a petition to beg the governor to send troops to protect them. A militia had also been hastily formed, and the little settlement sounded more like a camp than a peaceable trading town, the bugle call rousing them from their rest, and echoing more or less all day.

I found Lucy in a state of great alarm, having received intelligence of the massacre, and, knowing my propensity to see all I could, she was half afraid I might have been in it, and therefore a prisoner, the last sad news of the murdering of the prisoners not having as yet reached Wellington, though half an hour after the arrival of the ship in which I had a passage people were hurrying about, pale and anxious groups were consulting as to the best mode of proceeding, while others were busily arranging their affairs preparatory to making a run for it, caring little for the settlement or their neighbours, provided they could secure the safety of their own goods and lives.

In the midst of this Colonel Wakefield returned, and with him several magistrates and constables, who had accompanied him to the Wairoa, with the view of protecting or saving their countrymen, and unhappily too strongly confirmed the report; thus giving fresh impetus to the excitement and apprehension fast degenerating into a panic.

Wellington followed the example of Nelson. Petitions for troops were hastily drawn up and dispatched by express, one to the capital, one to Sydney, and one to Tasmania. This being done, the militia was called out, and commenced an energetic drilling. In short, every measure in the power of the company to maintain their position and keep the Maories in awe was put into requisition; and not certainly before it was necessary, as there had been a fresh influx of natives into the Hutt valley, who scrupled little whom they offended or insulted, or whose land they trespassed on, having one answer always ready, that "they were Rauparaha's men, not of the queen of the Pakehas."

Being a magistrate I found my hands pretty well occupied, and was obliged to leave poor Lucy a good deal alone, her health not permitting her to accompany me so often as her inclination prompted.

It was in the midst of this immediate excitement and anxiety that we heard of the sad loss of our dear friend the Rev. Mr.

Gray, who was drowned in attempting to ford a swollen stream not many miles from his station.

The account affected Lucy so deeply, that, taking into consideration the unprotected state of his poor wife and family, and moreover their very probable want of funds to remove to a safer locality, I determined to go at once and bring them all down to Wellington, where they could remain as our guests until arrangements for their future comfort could be made. At first Lucy would not hear of my doing so, but gradually gave in to a sense of the helpless position of the poor widow and her little children, surrounded as she was by natives.

I shall never forget the night preceding my departure. Lucy could not rest, and grew so nervous and ill, that I offered to give up the idea of the journey, and send some one instead of me; but this she in turn would not listen to, and made light of her own feelings, insisting upon my putting my first plan into execution.

My journey was by no means a comfortable or even safe one; not that I had any cause to fear an open assault from either Rauparaha or his followers, as, never having chanced to be brought into opposition with the natives in any way, I had no man's private revenge to dread, and was, as a government officer, perfectly secure, Rauparaha's policy being then to remain perfectly passive, and abide in pretended patience the decision of the Governor, whose arrival was daily anticipated. The great warrior himself was not at Otaki when I passed, but some little distance inland in a new pah, where, with his son-in-law and adviser, the Englishman I before mentioned, he was engaged superintending extensive fortifications, on a plan which afterwards excited the admiration of the military, and puzzled many a wise head.

I had a strong desire and curiosity to see Rauparaha, and trusting to the open professions of peace he took so much pains to promulgate,—and moreover, having an interest in the trade in flax, which many of the natives in the district had been carrying on under the direction of some Englishman—I determined to brave the lion in his den; and accordingly, under the pretext of getting a safe pass for Mrs. Gray and her family, I went direct to the upper pah, and demanded an interview with the dreaded Rauparaha himself. I found him settled in a clean, tidy-looking hut, the floor covered with handsome flax mats, and hung all round with guns, spears, &c.. He received me just outside the doorway in the presence of Ranghitana, Kauri, and one or two others of his principal warrior chiefs, never having seen any of whom, I could not of course gratify my curiosity as to which was the Englishman, the famous Kauri. Size and height were no guides, each of the men present being of about the same stature; all were wrapped in their blankets and seated, so that at a cursory glance, I could distinguish very little difference.

Rauparaha received me very politely, and much more affectionately than the occasion merited, at once acceding to my request, and offering an escort of warriors if I wished it, even shedding tears over Mr. Gray's fate, telling me, with uplifted eyes and hypocritical whine, that he was a missionary himself. This I afterwards found so far correct, that he had professed Christianity immediately after the Wairoa massacre, and regularly attended the chapel at Otaki, though only for the purpose of blinding the settlers and gaining over the converted natives to his cause.

Having satisfied my curiosity, I was on the point of departing, but the great man insisted upon my remaining the night, which was fast approaching, pointing at the same time to the dark and lowering clouds that were gathering, which being accompanied by intense heat and a peculiar breathless thickness of the atmosphere, proclaimed a coming storm, not a pleasant thing to meet in the open air if you can avoid it by staying under a weather-tight roof. Circumstanced as I was, it required very little pressing, and quietly taking out my pipe and 'baccy-pouch, proceeded to enjoy myself until supper-time. As Rauparaha glanced greedily at the fragrant weed I offered to replenish his pipe, and thereby brought a smile of gratitude to his ugly countenance. One or two others presently gave me pretty broad hints as to the appreciation of this same performance, so my pouch began to look rather lanky, and when it had gone the round of the circle, came back with barely a pipeful left.

A good cloud now curled upwards, ascending in spiral columns in the still air, the sounds in the pah were the only ones that disturbed the silence, until the sound of a sort of drum gave notice that the supper was prepared, and made me laugh as I thought of the contrast between the gong-like call to the savages' meal, which might be roasted human flesh for all I knew, and the sonorous roll of the gong in one of the autocrat halls of England.

Looking up, I caught a similar smile upon the tattooed face of one of the chiefs, and by one of those strange impulses of thought which sometimes strike one almost supernaturally, I at once came to the conclusion that this was Kauri. Having a strong notion, however, that if he suspected any such suspicion regarding himself my life would not be worth an hour's purchase, I controlled the impulse to express my opinion, and turned away determined to watch and at the same time to be on my guard not to attract his suspicions.

It soon became a fixed idea in my mind I had seen this man before, though where or when I could not imagine. In vain I tried to bring the time to my remembrance. One thing, however, I was sure of, that *I had met him*, and that *he, too, recognised me*; that he had been tattooed since I saw him might account for my being unable to recognise him; but though I could feel his eye upon me constantly, I could not catch either it or the sound of his voice, anxiously as I tried, and I started without speaking to him. Still I had gained something, for I felt sure I should be able to recognise him again, having carefully noted some peculiarities in the designs tattooed on his face. I had been determined to do my best to bring him to justice before I saw him; but now the wish became stronger than ever; it haunted me night and day. By the time I got up to poor Gray's station, I became convinced that there was some link between us, and that he and I must stand face to face again in the dire conflict for dear life.

My journey from Otaki to the Wanganui was a very weary one, the weather being oppressively close, thunder rolling like distant guns, and yet not a drop of rain or breath of wind to cool the furnace-like atmosphere. Once or twice I fancied I felt the sensation of an earthquake, and paused to wait for its coming again, but in vain. When I reached the Wanganui I found the inhabitants in the utmost alarm and consternation, four or five smart shocks of an earthquake having taken place, each increasing in severity; and although no damage had as yet been done, there was no appearance of any change in the aspect of the weather, and every one was nervously expecting a greater shock than had yet been felt.

I was too tired with my walk (having pushed on very fast in the night to gain comfortable quarters) to pay so much attention to their anticipations as I should otherwise have been inclined to do, and after a hearty meal, lay down to get much required sleep. I had scarcely given my wearied limbs their preparatory stretch, when I felt the earth begin to rock, with a short, unpleasant motion, causing almost simultaneously a feeling akin to intense sea-sickness, which increased as I sprang to my feet, and ran into the open air, where pale, frightened groups were ranged about in every attitude and degree of terror. For, believe me, the bravest heart will quail at such terrible crumbling and tumbling of the solid earth. I have seen one who has led men against an overwhelming force of his country's enemies, and charged into the very mouths of the enemy's guns without a quicker throb in his heart, cover his face and shudder like a child at the sound of God's thunder. The little children and natives alone took the phenomenon coolly, one from ignorance, the other from custom, earthquakes being very frequent, often coming on very suddenly, and seldom doing any real mischief.

Several smart shocks next followed, each smarter than before. The river bubbled angrily, rising as if flooded. Presently a breeze sprang up, the trembling in the ground ceased, and settlers began to regain their equanimity and courage, and to talk of earthquakes as if of every day occurrence.

CHAPTER VI.

A RIDE BY MOONLIGHT.

WHILE waiting at the Wanganui for the arrival of a vessel to carry us on to Wellington, I fell in with a sort of land speculator, and Jack-of-all-trades, whose quaint manners and good-natured roughness excited a curiosity to know more of him. I soon found that, though rather difficult to understand in the outset, he was a first-rate fellow at heart, and a man of birth and education to boot; having visited most parts of the world, and traded more or less in all, he could give me a fund of information. Nothing seemed to have escaped him. The politics of the day, the changes in the ministry for the last five or six years, the phases through which the Company had passed, these were all familiar topics. He had seen everything, and seemed to know every one I mentioned. And when in speaking of my early experiences of the colony and the North—on which subject he questioned me pretty closely—I inadvertently alluded to my meeting with Trevor, I could see by his attention I had hit upon a congenial subject; and thinking I might learn something of my friend, I went on talking of him more warmly than I might otherwise have done.

"Ah!" exclaimed the stranger, interrupting me, "you've no idea what his real name is, I suppose? He didn't tell you, did he?"

"No—how should I? I never thought of it. In fact, it never struck me he had given me a false one."

"Ah! strange—strange, indeed! Trevor is a friend—at least, an acquaintance of mine: met him for the first time at a small dinner given by his Royal Highness the Prince Regent. I met him the second time in the convict hospital at Botany Bay; and I met him for the third and last time in the ante-room at the new Governor's *levée* a few weeks ago. Strange! truly strange!" and he took a pinch of snuff in a noisy manner, evidently to relieve his feelings.

"You look surprised, so am I. Trevor will tell you why, I dare say, if you ask him some day. Tell him 'the doctor' made your acquaintance, and intends to be your friend;

that is to say, if you will permit him to be so."

He held out his hand, which I took, setting him down in my private opinion as little short of a madman, especially with regard to the ideality of the Prince Regent.

"Trevor is on the point of leaving the colony; some private and very important affairs are taking him home. I suppose you saw enough to make you guess he was under a cloud. That being the case, as I judge by your attention and countenance, you will be glad to hear he is likely to have the matter, whatever it may be, that sent him out of England, cleared up. His punishment—I mean his absence—now will be optional. It is probable you will see him previously to his trip to the other side of the world. He mentioned to me that he was coming to Wellington. By the by, do you happen to know anything as to the whereabouts of a fellow named Black, in whom our friend takes some interest?"

I shook my head.

"No? That's a pity. I have a curiosity to see him. There's some little private feud between him and you, is there not?"

I was a little startled. He evidently knew more of me than he acknowledged, and was in Trevor's confidence regarding my private affairs.

Now I never consider it a pleasant thing to fall in with a person (whose very existence has been hitherto unknown to you), and find your life, actions, aspirations, fears and hopes, are all familiar subjects in their eyes; therefore I was not altogether pleased with this accurate acquaintance with my affairs, and betrayed the same when I replied to his question, for, with a strange amused smile, he laid his hand upon my shoulder, saying, in a soothing, kindly voice—

"Don't get angry with Trevor; he's the best friend you'll find out here. Try to please him when you meet him again. You'll never regret it. Don't forget my advice, young man; some day you may thank me for it. Trevor is an extraordinary man. Had he been more fortunate, or rather less unfortunate on the threshhold of life, he would have made a figure in the world. As it is, he had better, like many of us, have been suffered to die during teething."

There was something so comical in his expression, that in spite of the application to my friend, I laughed.

"Ah! you laugh. Well, it's true, though. It's a pity the nurse cannot read the future in a baby's face, and act accordingly. But talking of babies, you are married; but I suppose the consummation of married happiness has not arrived yet? Where did you pick up your 'help-meet?' Trevor was considerably surprised; rather put out on the whole, and had some extravagant idea that you'd made a mess of it, until some friends of yours turned up in the Governor's suite, and said you'd married a Colonel Somebody's daughter."

"I married Colonel Sinclair's second daughter."

"Not poor Alick Sinclair who was drowned in Lake Taupo?"

"Yes, his daughter Lucy."

"By Jupiter! you're a lucky fellow. I nearly married her myself. Nay, don't be jealous. I thought better of it before I proposed, and remembered the song of May and December. But, joking apart, Lucy was one of the sweetest children I ever saw, and the light of her poor father's life. What a sudden fate his was. I believe there was a party of them?"

So I enlightened him as to the sad story, which he did not altogether know, having been in Sydney when the accident happened. He was very much affected, and told me the Colonel and he had been friends at school, then college, and afterwards through life; indeed, that it was principally by his advice that the Colonel settled in New Zealand.

Next morning I found my extraordinary acquaintance had taken his departure, leaving a message that he would meet me at Wellington, though when I reached home he was again on the wing. Lucy had seen a good deal of him, and was full of conjectures and curiosity regarding Trevor, proposing such wonderful solutions to the mystery, that after a few days his name became a household word among us.

The spring was now verging into summer. The native disputes had given place for a while to the more pressing duties of seed-sowing and planting. An enterprising individual had started an omnibus between Wellington and the Hutt, which ran, or rather jolted over a road that would have shaken the mental *capacity* of a Londoner as much as it shook the digestive organs of the Wellingtonians who ventured their lives and bones in its charge. A great part of the Hutt was now partially, if not wholly, cleared, the natives having worked so energetically on their side since Rauparaha's assumption of authority, that they had met the settlers half-way; and although much had been said as to making a definite boundary, nothing had been done; and considerable fears were entertained as to the fate of some of the young crops, from the marauding propensities of the sheep and pigs owned by the Maori farmers, which pigs, never having been subjected to control by their owners, were obliged to be herded off by the settlers themselves, thus adding an extra expense. Some few of them had tried the plan of erecting hedges or rails; but this looked too much like making a boundary, and as it happened that the natives had made extensive encroachments, it was deemed imprudent to give the slightest appearance to their appropriated ground. So the settlers pulled down their fences again, and hired boys or girls to hound off the intruders.

I had been somewhat disappointed in not hearing from or seeing Trevor, especially after the hopes held out by "the doctor." Dick Hyde, it is true, had written, saying that it was by his advice he had taken a piece of ground, about three miles from Auckland, which, having been partially cleared by its first owner, was in a fair way to pay any outlay, even during the first year. He added that it was lucky he had come then, as Trevor was leaving the country, and had given him up furniture and implements he did not require any longer; so Dick was all enthusiasm both with Trevor and himself. Moreover, very satisfactory letters from "home" had been brought by one of the new Governor's staff, so that there was little wonder he was in first-rate spirits, ending his epistle by advising me to come and pay him a visit.

"Shall we?" asked Lucy, as she read the letter over my shoulder. "Mr. Hyde is such a merry creature, I think he'd do us both good. For really, Martin, since you came back from the Wanganui you've scarcely smiled."

"Upon my word, Lucy, you are too bad; I never felt so contentedly happy in my life. Everything has been going on so quietly and comfortably, and now you propose breaking it all up by a long, wearisome voyage to Auckland. Besides, I don't think it would be altogether prudent for you under the circumstances."

Lucy blushed, and looked a little disappointed.

"Then promise me that you'll take me as soon as I can go?"

"Certainly, if you wish it; but at present you must nurse your dear little self, and—— Why, Loo! what's the matter? You have tears in your eyes."

"Nothing, nothing, darling. I'm nervous, I think. Such strange thoughts flash across me, sometimes. I cannot tell how or why they come, but I cannot altogether banish them."

"What kind of thoughts, Loo? You surely can tell me. Perhaps telling them may frighten them away."

But Lucy shook her head.

"No, no, pet! let me keep them to myself. They are little trials, I suppose, to make me keep a guard upon my mind. You love me, don't you, Martin?"

"Love you, Loo! What can make you ask me such a question? Love you, my own dear wife! Whom on earth can I love but you? If you ask me such a silly question again I shall be obliged to send for the doctor, and tell him about these thoughts of yours. He must exorcise the ghost, or whatever it is."

The bright drops were, however. still in Lucy's eyes, and when, after joking and petting her until I had brought smiles to her lips, I left the room, and having to ride to the head of the Hutt, was soon cantering along the beach, my thoughts were too busy with Lucy to let my attention travel elsewhere, or I should have saved myself an aching heart, and many an anxious hour.

My ride was destined to be longer than I intended, as on reaching the land I was to look over I found the owner at an outlying station, some six miles into the bush. Not caring to have the ride over again next day, and there being a bright moon, I pushed on at a hand-gallop, found my friend, got through my business, and started on my homeward road just after nine o'clock, the full moon showing everything almost as light as day.

I had not ridden above a couple of miles when my horse stumbled, and before I could recover him he was down. Although shaken, I had luckily fallen safely, and after a twist or two to see that no bones were out of order, I prepared to mount again. But just as I did so my foot became entangled in something, and putting down my hand I caught hold of a line, which I presently found stretched across the road.

This, then, had been the cause of my mishap, accident it certainly was not. My first impulse was to pull out my pistol, and stand ready for an attack, imagining that the string had been laid by some one, who thought I might have something worth lightening my pocket of. I looked anxiously round, peering into the dark shade made by the overhanging bushes, and listening intensely for any sound, but I heard nothing. In the confusion of the moment I had forgotten that the snare could scarcely have been intended for me, I having gone by a different road, and in consequence of my ride being extended much further to the west than I expected, I had taken this, the nearest way to Wellington.

While these thoughts were running, or rather flashing, through my mind, a shrill whistle rang up the valley, and was answered so close to me that I must confess I felt my heart perform the feat that is commonly described as "leaping up into one's mouth." At the same instant a handkerchief was passed over my head, the pistol knocked out of my hand before I could make the slightest resistance, and I was thrown on my face, and my arms pinioned. The whole thing being accomplished as quickly as I can tell it, and to my disgust and indignation there I lay, perfectly helpless, and at the mercy of my assailants, whoever they might happen to be.

A few minutes (they seemed hours to me) passed. Not a word had been spoken as yet, and I might have thought the whole proceeding to be imagination, but for my helplessness, and the suppressed breathing of two or three human beings. At last I was lifted, carried a short way, and then laid down.

Some one sat by my head, and amused themselves by occasionally laying the cold blade of a knife upon my cheek, by way, I presume, of keeping me quiet; and truly it was a most effectual, if not a pleasant method. My powers of locomotion were limited enough without such an unnecessary reminder. And the cold steel sent a chill through my veins that made my blood absolutely curdle and creep.

How long I remained in this state it would be hard to say. Suddenly the intense silence was broken by the sound of several horses galloping, accompanied with loud voices and laughter. An expression of satisfaction broke from the watcher beside me, which, to my surprise, was that of a woman, though whether native or English I could not then determine.

Nearer and nearer came the voices of the unconscious victims, and quicker, too, grew the suppressed breathing of the woman beside me, whose trembling eagerness had something so fiendish that I almost forgot the fate awaiting the riders in a sort of fascination of curiosity.

On they came; they were within earshot, when a clear voice, I recognised with a thrill of horror as Trevor's, exclaimed—

"It's not a bad country if——"

Then came a crash and loud voices, pistol shots, and cries; but over all rang a shriek from the woman, as, springing up, and totally forgetful of me, she rushed into the *melée.*

I was left alone!

Now was my chance to escape and break my bonds. So, stretching every muscle, and regardless of pain, I struggled on until the thong that encircled my hands was wrenched away. The rest was comparatively easy. As the covering fell from my face I saw a dark mass fighting and struggling in the road beneath me.

I hesitated only for a moment as to whether I should try to help, or take refuge in flight. The reader must not set me down as a coward for entertaining any doubt as to what course I should pursue. I was perfectly unarmed, my arms and hands stiff and torn in getting off my fetters, and a painful sensation in my ankle reminding me of my fall. My hesitation was of little importance. A second party of travellers was approaching, evidently unexpected by the assailants, who now, finding they would have the worst of it, made an attempt to escape. Three of them managed to effect this; but two remained prisoners, one mortally wounded, the other with the charge from Trevor's pistol in his leg.

The meeting between Trevor and myself was one of pleasure to both of us; we seemed fated to meet in strange ways, this last, however, the most mysterious of all, as nothing we could conjecture threw the slightest light upon the proceedings, unless, indeed, Trevor's party had been mistaken for a Government one; this supposition was strengthened by the fact that he had not told any one of his intention to visit Wellington. He had spent the preceding night at the camp or pah of Rauparaha, and only left it at mid-day, being advised to push on by the chief himself, on some trivial pretext as to the weather, or something of the kind. On his way he had fallen in with a party of settlers, fortunately, too, for him, as, if alone, there was no doubt he would have been murdered at once.

To ride on to Wellington as speedily as possible, give the alarm, and send out a body of the volunteer police was now the wisest thing, as the natives—for such the men who had attacked us seemed to be—would probably gather a larger party, and attempt to rescue the fellow in our hands.

I would have taken Trevor home with me, but he had already accepted the offer of accommodation from Frank Webster, one of the settlers he had met with. So, arranging to meet him next morning, I left them at the entrance to the town, feeling too stiff to care about the further exertion of going to the police magistrate, who, I may as well mention, was no friend of mine, and treated the whole matter so lightly, that he got very little favour from the colonists afterwards.

It seems that just after I had left home that afternoon a native appeared, and demanded to see me. Not content with Lucy's report of my absence, he had remained prowling about until a white woman joined him, when they went away together.

CHAPTER VII.

CLARI HAS A SECRET TO TELL ME.

TREVOR gave me no clue to the cause of his departure from New Zealand. He hinted that he meant to return eventually, but the when was uncertain. He gave me advice as to settling, offering me money if I required it, made me promise to write regularly by each mail, addressing to the care of my own agents, whence he said he could easily procure the letters.

He gave me a packet of papers, &c.,

which he stated to be of value in my hands, to be opened and made use of by me in case of his death, telling me he had left me all he had to leave, and that in the packet I should find an account of my father's life, which, in the event of anything ever happening to bring the circumstances before the public, would tend to clear him from blame.

During his visit he won Lucy's respect and affection, and the night before his departure he spoke long and earnestly of my happiness in possessing such a wife, warning me to attend to her every wish or weakness, to avoid even the shadow of a wrong, and remember my mother's fate.

Johnson having been absent on business at Nelson, they did not meet, though I found the latter had been very anxious to accomplish it, having fallen in with Mr.

Halket, the strange character mentioned in a preceding chapter, and from him heard some things regarding Trevor, which strongly excited his curiosity.

Nothing further transpired as to the outrage I had very nearly been a victim of in the Hutt. Rauparaha was still near the Manakan, building, fortifying, and gasconading to his heart's content, openly branding the English as cowards, insulting the whole Government, and all this with the most perfect impunity, no one taking any measures to put a stop to his bragging or lying, but making the best excuse they could seize upon, namely, that they were waiting for the new governor. The advent of the new governor was a subject of great importance, and as the time that must necessarily elapse before an answer could be obtained from England drew to a close; the conjectures and excitement became intense, nothing else was listened to or talked of, and every sail that came in sight brought crowds of news-hunters down to the beach. December, however, came, and summer and all its festivities were at their height, when at last we heard the long-expected answer, and were told that a Captain Fitzroy, late of the royal navy, had been sent out to fill the important post. There was a general feeling of disappointment and disgust. Not, indeed, that we knew anything against the capacity of Captain Fitzroy at that time, but simply that the appointment was felt to be of such importance that a more experienced man ought to have been chosen, and it was not likely that this new man could have gained any experience as a colonist on board a man of war. Still the Company hoped that, coming out unprejudiced, he might happen to look more fairly upon the Company, and try to amalgamate the whole society of the colony.

The moderation and wisdom evinced by the Bishop had already won the admiration and affection of most of the colonists, and the general belief was, that if he judged boldly for himself, the *clerical* influence in New Zealand would become what it ought to be.

Excitement now took the place of expectation. And as many of the settlers as could afford it, set off for Auckland, while the very nativès began to look anxious, and Rauparaha edged on towards Taupo, sending his friends or emissaries into all parts of the country to prepare them for anything that might happen.

The first news that reached us was

that Lieutenant Shortland had thrown up his appointment, having been openly insulted by Governor Fitzroy, at the first levée. This did not surprise many, as Shortland was not a very popular man, though on the whole he had acted well and straightforwardly.

The other state-servants remained for the meanwhile in their various offices, though they were warned it was only on sufferance, and might be changed any day in case of their doing anything which might declare against their several capacities.

Ever since the formation of Wellington, Christmas and New Year had been kept up as strictly as possible in accordance with those festive and happy seasons in England. And, although they here fell in the warmth of Midsummer, when the whole country is teeming with fruit, flowers, and foliage, we always decked the interior of the houses with green things, and by inviting friends, and eating beef and plum-pudding, tried to cheat ourselves into thinking they were just like the Christmas days in England. The churches were also decorated and service held.

A boat-race came off one day, horse-racing, and games, another, while picnics, balls, dinners, and fêtes made up the programme from Christmas Eve to Twelfth Night, after which the Wellingtonians began to breathe again, the Hutt settlers, &c., to return to their farms, and the whole community to find time to discuss the new Governor, and wonder what he had been about since he was lost sight of in the gaiety of the season.

Lucy had been a quiet spectatress of all the amusements, taking as much part as she could, but still acting as the main-spring to the pleasantest gatherings.

Johnson was again almost constantly with us, the temporary estrangement having passed away imperceptibly; indeed ended to all appearance in bringing us more together. And as my increasing business took me more away from home than formerly; and the medical men told me my wife must not be permitted to brood over the sad events of her past, I was rather glad to see him ready to cater for her amusement, and thankful that the shadow I had noticed awhile ago, was vanishing from her face.

One day, towards the latter part of December, a native stopped me on my way to the Hutt, and after looking mysteriously all about, to see if we were alone, handed me a letter.

To my amazement I found it was from Clari. She was ill, dying she said; nothing could save her life; and yet she could not die until she had seen me, and communicated a secret which was of the utmost importance to me. I read, and re-read the faint lines, trying to gather something more than they really expressed, and uncertain how to proceed, or what answer to send by the messenger, who, having crept under a bush near, lay with his bright eyes fixed eagerly on my face.

I beckoned to him, and as he sprang up, something in his manner and movements struck me as familiar.

"I have seen you before, friend," I said. "Ah! I remember. You are bold, or cunning, to come here; which is it?"

Though the question was a mere chance guess, the shot told. Crouching down beside my horse, he whined out a prayer for my forgiveness and pity, telling me he did not know who it was when he threw me down.

"Ha!" I exclaimed, almost betraying myself in my surprise at the confession he had let escape him of being one of the party who had waylaid Trevor; "ha! a line is the work of cowards; a brave man goes up to his enemy and strikes. Rauparaha's children fight in the dark like women and wild beasts."

"Ha! ha!" he laughed, "woman fight for love and hate. The Maori girl cannot be like the white one. It was well for the stranger that he bıoke his bonds. He would have kissed colder things than his wife's lips. But let the letter be answered; the sun is going down, and the pah is many miles away."

"Does the girl think me a fool? Tell her the thongs were sharp, and that my flesh is still sore."

"The Pakeha must come," he said, in a marked tone. "There is no danger; Rauparaha is a brother of the settler, and the letter is from his pah. The girl will send for the Pakeha's wife, if he refuse to come."

I read the letter again. Could the secret be anything connected with Black, who, though I had been unable to trace or hear of, I firmly believed to be still in the country? Or perhaps it was of Trevor, who seemed to know more of her than he had explained to me? So I determined to go, feeling that I could guard against dangers on the way, and when once in Rauparaha's pah I was perfectly safe, he being at that time especially on his good behaviour.

I turned and rode home, half inclined to explain the whole thing to Lucy, and tell her my reasons for going away. Unfortunately I found her with Mrs. Gray, and like many a good intention, lost or put aside by a chance, or, at least, what to our eyes appears a chance interruption, I deferred the explanation, saying I had some business that would take me to the Otaki district. Lucy knew I had employed the natives there in flax-dressing, and asked no questions.

The preparations for my journey did not occupy very much time, so I was several miles on my way by nightfall, and the following evening reached the village of Otaki. I rode direct to old Dennis's hut, where I knew I should be able to get a shake down for the night. I found him perfectly helpless, and worn almost to a shadow. He did not recognise me in the least this time, looking vacantly up, muttering his poor child's name over and over again. Poor old man! he died soon after, and without recovering his senses.

The settlement at Otaki was increasing in size and importance, and at that period promised to attract a larger population than the Wanganui, which, however, shortly after took the lead, and far eclipsed the older settlement. This was partly attributable to the decrease in the whale trade, partly to the ill-feeling that sprang up between the settlers and the natives, which leading to thefts, and even in some cases murder, deterred emigrants from settling there.

All the good that existed was, I believe, entirely attributable to Archdeacon Hadfield, whose influence over the natives more than once saved not only the Otaki settlement, but Wellington itself. And had there been more of such men in New Zealand, we should have heard nothing of wars or disunion between the emigrants and natives. A true Christian gentleman, brave as a lion, yet meek and gentle as a child, possessing talents of the highest order, and a highly cultivated mind, kind, firm, and impartial, utterly forgetful of selfish advantages, and unwearied in well-doing, Octavius Hadfield won deservedly the respect and love of all who came under his influence.

The natives knew and acknowledged that he had their true advancement and happiness at heart, and that all he did was out of consideration for the peace and prosperity of the country to which he had given his life and labour. He won their confidence and affection by the interest he took in all concerning them, never resting content until he had made every new movement of the government or settlers clear to their comprehension, gradually engrafting them with a desire to increase their personal and domestic comforts, and imitate the civilization of their English brethren, impressing them with a sense of their religious obligations, and of the true happiness they would attain, not only hereafter but here, by adhering to the laws of the Almighty, and having perfect faith in his wisdom.

His plan was not so much to preach as to talk to them, putting in a word as occasion required. And there seemed something like inspiration in the application he made of events of the moment, the commonest objects and most trivial things being made the medium of conveying the highest and mightiest truths. With him truly one felt there was nothing too small to be of importance, nothing that the Almighty had deemed worthy to create, that was not worthy our care and attention. Divine wisdom seemed to guide him in his ministry, and teach him how to mingle the gradual change from their old superstition to the true and enlightened faith of the Christian. He felt, what unfortunately few of the clergymen in the colony have seemed to appreciate, that he had men made after God's image to deal with, minds as capable of understanding, and cultivation as our own; men whose reason must be satisfied before they could be moulded to a new form, and whose belief must be gained by the power of conviction, not by force.

Acknowledging the hand of God in the unlettered and primitive man, his doctrine and practice was to build on the foundation laid by the Almighty, with the materials given by inspiration, imitating as much as human intellect can, *the gradual development worked out by Divine Power.*

To every man who wishes to be a missionary I would point to Archdeacon Hadfield and say,

" Go thou and do likewise."

I found Rauparaha had removed further nland, and consequently had to obtain a guide, not exactly knowing the position of the pah he then occupied, and not wishing to run the risk of missing my way and putting off my time.

The weather, which had been very calm and fine, now suddenly broke up, and the day following my arrival at Otaki, a storm of wind and rain came on, more violent than any I had witnessed in the colony.

People in England have no idea what wind is in New Zealand. It does not come in gusts, as in England, or in a tornado, as in tropical countries; but rather like a heavy though imperceptible body, acting with a steady even pressure, accompanied by a hollow sighing sound, breaking into shrieks and roars when opposed by trees, or any other palpable object. It does not, as might be supposed from a description, overthrow or tear up and destroy, as a much less amount of strength when coming in gusts in other countries often does. Trees do not *rend* but *bend*, the slighter trees stooping gracefully before it, then rising again as fresh and beautiful as before. True, fruit trees suffer, and that often severely; but as the winds are always expected, and it is known they will come, and generally about the same time, and from the same quarter, people are in a measure prepared for them, and able to guard against their influence.

The wind, succeeding my arrival, completely put a stop to any possibility of my accomplishing my journey that day. So I was fain to stay where I was. However, I made a fair start next morning, and reached the pah at midday.

The country round had been cleared in several places, and wheat crops waved yellow in the autumn sun, giving the promise of an ample harvest. Some of the inclosures held small flocks of sheep, others were planted with potatoes and maize. These fields were bounded with thick flax plantations, from some parts of which rose large forest trees. The pah itself was carefully surrounded by a high fence of boughs, &c. perfectly impervious to sight. Over this the columns of smoke rising, betokened the presence of a considerable number of inhabitants; and as I drew nearer, small savoury whiffs of roast pork betokened a feast, and some unusual festival, the natives never indulging in such luxuries save on special occasions, either the arrival of guests, the anniversary of a great victory, or some such marked occurrence.

I was immediately conducted to the hut of Rauparaha, and welcomed by him. Though quite alone when he received me, the hut was soon filled with natives, all eager to shake hands, and remind me of the tobacco I had distributed on the occasion of my first visit, some of them venturing to show me their appreciation by holding their pipes ostentatiously before me, and loudly expressing their admiration of my former generosity, and not only mine either, but adding a large dose of soft sawder' anent the English nation in general.

Having presented a small piece of the grateful weed to the most important warriors, I requested to be taken to the hut of Clari, whose message I had repeated to Rauparaha as the cause of my visit. Half-a-dozen fellows started forward to show me the way; but Rauparaha put them aside, and taking my arm in imitation of the fashion he had seen at Wellington, waved them all back, and led me through a labyrinth of cooking houses, stores, &c. to a large and well-built hut, across the door of which hung a white curtain, and from which came every now and then a suppressed moan of agony.

CHAPTER VIII.

DEATH OF CLARI.

At first I scarcely recognised in the deathlike and attenuated form lying upon a heap of mats, the woman I had last seen in the prime of life and beauty. She had made an effort to sit up, when I appeared, but sunk back with a groan, and beckoned me to come to her side.

"I am dying, Martin," she said, in a scarcely audible voice. "You wonder at my sending for you. I must be quick, and tell you why, or *he* will be back, and then I dare not; if he had not been absent I dare not have sent for you."

"Who?" I asked, as she stopped to recover breath.

"Black."

"Black! Is he here? In the pah?"

"Not to-day, or you would not see me. He was afraid to see me die, the coward and fiend that he is, and when I grew worse he went away. But he is not far off, and if he hears I have sent for you he will come. I have something to tell you, Martin. I swore I would never do so, but the devil is in my soul, and I must tell you before he will leave me. I have enough to answer for—— give me a drink or I shall choke."

I got up and brought a cup of water holding it to her lips as she gulped down a few mouthfuls.

"There. sit down——be quick——I have not much time. My heart is bursting with this agony."

"Do not speak, Clari," I said, "I care not to hear anything if it is pain to you. Rest quietly; perhaps in an hour or two you may feel calmer."

She laughed a low wild laugh that made me shudder.

"An hour or two, boy! In an hour or two I shall stand before the judgment; and if I carry my secret away with me, you may live to curse the day you were born. Hush! what is that?"

I listened but heard nothing. She too, listened, her eyes glaring wildly, and a bright red spot kindling in each cheek.

"It is nothing, but I must begin. Your mother, Martin, you remember her?"

"Yes, what of her?" I exclaimed.

"Patience!—she was separated from your father,—deserted by him, if you like it better."

"Do you know anything more?"

"Yes; God forgive him, I know it all."

"All?" she cried, in a shrill tone, half rising up, "all? liar! you do not, you could not know all. You could not come here to mock me in my last hour. You could——"

She paused, her eyes dilating and fixed upon the entrance. I could see nothing, though I sprang up and looked out of the hut.

"Hush!" she whispered, seizing my hand and pulling me down until my face was on a level with her own—"he's there, but I'll tell you. Yes, yes, fiend! devil incarnate! I'll tell him," she shrieked again, looking at the entrance, and clutching me with the force of a maniac.

"Listen, Martin! the man they call Black is—" she sprang up with a terrible cry as the report of a pistol discharged close at my ear almost stunned me.

Dropping her hand I rushed out, but no one except a native woman was near, sitting as I had seen her before, with her face covered in her blanket. The murderer must have concealed himself with almost supernatural speed. For that he had been inside the hut, the report of the pistol was evidence.

Clari lay half off the mat, a stream of blood issuing from a bullet-wound in her forehead. I lifted her up, but she was quite dead, and the secret whatever it was, was sealed by the awful hand of death.

For a few minutes I stood looking at the features, so terribly distorted by the momentary struggle, the expression of fear and hatred stiffening indelibly upon them. I was roused by Rauparaha himself taking my arm.

"The spirit has gone, friend; come away; the missionary can do no more for her."

Hastily, and as clearly as possible, I detailed the circumstances of her death; and he evinced so little surprise or indignation at such an outrage taking place in the heart of his own encampment, that I could only explain it by supposing him to have sanctioned the act. In vain I remonstrated, pointing out the crime, the investigation due, and the assurance that I would leave nothing untried to discover the perpetrator. To my amazement he smiled answering,

"You had better be careful friend. There was no one with her but yourself. And I can swear, now I am a missionary, the woman was bad; let her die, it is better so. You have a wife; did you speak to her of Clari? The passing clouds can be seen, but passing thoughts cannot be seen. Look you, friend, I will tell you the story of a Maori, it will show you what you can do."

"A great chief of the Nga-pius had a son, he had also one daughter, beautiful as the spring. To her came many lovers, but she turned from them, until Tutei appeared. Then her heart grew full, her eyes melted, trembling she listened to his voice. After many days he came to her brother's house and said,

"'Give me your sister, Atuahua to be my wife.'

"But the brother did not like Tutei, and spoke harshly, bidding him seek another wife. Then Tutei went away to his own friends and married a wife.

"When Atuahua heard of it, the light left her eyes, she sat down silently in the hut. Her brother came to comfort her, but she turned away.

"At last she sent for him, and said, 'call a messenger, and bid him bring Tutei to me. I cannot die until I see him once again. So her brother sent, and found Tutei, who was in the house of his wife, who loved him, and whom he loved.

"He was sitting at his wife's feet when the messenger came, who being a wise man, and knowing that jealousy is parent to murder, he stood aside until Tutei was alone; and Tutei hid it from his wife, thinking why should I vex her. Atuahua is dying, and a stranger. Therefore I shall be most merciful if I bury the thing in my own heart. So he made an excuse to his wife, and hastened across the mountains to see Atuahua.

She was dead; and he returned, grief written in his face.

"When his wife questioned him, he opened his heart, and told her of his former love. She listened patiently, and said nothing; so Tutei thought all was well. But in the darkness of night he was awakened from his rest by a sharp pain. He rose, and knew he was wounded, and that the blood was running away with his life. He tried to rise, but his feet were fastened. He heard his wife breathe beside him, and called out. She laughed, and said, 'She whom thou hast loved, hast called thee; peace! be happy; I have sent thee to her. But, Tutei, deceive her not, or perhaps she will not be so kind.' So Tutei bled to death, and his spirit departed to seek her he had once loved so well; so it is, the heart of woman cannot believe in the largeness of man's heart, friend. They will be one, or they care not to be there at all. I have had many wives, friend, and they are all alike. Go back to thy companion, I say, and keep silence. The other is silent in the grave; let her be. It is well. Rauparaha can give no better words."

We entered his hut as he concluded this harangue, he having cleverly timed his narrative according to our walk. Mats were laid out, and several chiefs ranged round, evidently waiting our approach. Among them I at once caught sight of Kauri, my eyes falling upon his face as one familiar, and one, too, that seemed to recall an indefinite period of my life. I soon found he had been absent, and, from what I could learn, upon a very important mission, namely, to secure the good will and alliance of Hohe Heki, the great hero of the north, and son-in-law of the well-known Hongi.

It was in vain I attempted to gain some information touching Black from Rauparaha. He affected perfect ignorance, and cleverly turned the subject whenever I attempted to refer to him. At last I gave up the attempt, determining, however, that I should not leave the pah until I had satisfied myself more fully both as to the cause of Clari's death and the whereabouts of the man whom I believed guilty of her murder, fearing she would betray the secret to which he now alone held the key.

The arrival of the new governor was a subject upon which the most intense interest was manifested. They questioned me eagerly as to my knowledge of his policy and opinions, expressing their disapproval of my guarded answer rather loudly, Rangihaeta becoming so violent that Rauparaha had to call him to order, and finally dismiss the meeting, not caring that I should see his son-in-law "bounce" any louder.

There was no use attempting any further remonstrance with Rauparaha, or telling him I meant to bury Clari and find out her murderer. He only laughed, asking me what power the forest-tree had against the axe of the settler, and bidding me be thankful that I had escaped the ball that killed her. Finding I was only wasting time in talking I turned away, and without taking the old hypocrite's outstretched hand, walked off. The Rev. Mr. Hadfield was absent from Otaki, and not being expected to return for several days, I could not obtain his help, but determined to return upon the first opportunity and seek his advice.

In spite of Rauparaha's story, I meant to give Lucy, as soon as her strength permitted, a clear account of the whole proceeding; but, alas! "man proposes," and "God disposes." I found Lucy very ill, and only got home an hour before the birth of the long-looked-for little one. A few short hours terminated his untimely taste of life; and though at the moment my anxiety for his mother made me callous to any feeling for him, in after times his wax-like face and wailing cry haunted many a lonely hour, and still often rise before me when called upon by a happy young mother to admire her new treasure.

Lucy was very ill, and though excessive danger passed away, her strength did not come again as it ought to have done. She never smiled or spoke of living, and any mention of the past brought such a painful look in her eyes, that I learnt to avoid that too.

At last, after a few months' anxiety I appealed to the doctor. He could find no disease, he said; the cause of illness must be mental, and for that the only advice he could offer complete change.

That very day I received a letter from Sydney upon business matters, which would obviously be better answered verbally; so hurrying home, I broke the news to Lucy, told her of the doctor's advice as to change, the advantage I should gain by attending to my business in Sydney myself, and the favourable opportunity it would afford for adopting the doctor's advice.

"Thank you, Martin, I am better here," was her answer, as she turned away from me.

"Lucy, darling, to please me; think a little, dear. Do not grieve over the poor baby. It was God's will. He may give us another; and the other is happier."

The tears ran silently down her pale face, but she said nothing.

"You must come, Loo; your health is the first consideration with me, and I cannot bear to see you looking so miserable. If you love me, Loo, you will come willingly."

"Love you, Martin!" broke from her lips in such a passionate tone of reproach, that the words rang in my ears for hours after. She hid her face in her hands, and leant it upon the table, before which she was sitting. Suddenly she looked up, and said—

"Martin, I am going to ask you a favour."

The blood rushed to my heart. Why should she call anything from me a favour? Surely some change had come, something had been creeping in between us; not, surely, the spirit of our buried little one; his pure spirit could only bring love and healing, not this painful and mysterious something. I rose from the stool I had taken at her side, and trying to look and speak calmly, said—

"I never said nay yet, Loo. Your pleasure has, I think I may honestly say, been mine."

She flushed, and for an instant her eyes turned inquiringly, and, as it seemed, upbraidingly on mine; then the same listless expression returned, and taking up her work, she began folding it.

"I was only going to ask if you had any objections to my asking Miny Millard to come and pay me a visit?"

The question took me by surprise: the thought struck me, could Miny have had anything to do with the change? I knew how deep and incomprehensible the workings of the heart are, and how buried thoughts, whose graves have long been covered with grass and flowers, will, after long years, seem to restore their dead, and permit their ghosts to haunt our happiest moments; that forgotten voices will at times return as familiar tones; that fears or pains we imagined conquered will rise in hours of weakness, and sting us to the soul. Memory may be guided, but never blinded. I had forgotten to answer Lucy until she repeated the question. Then going to her, I put my arms round her, looking into her eyes as cheerfully as I could as I said—

"Certainly, Lucy; but if I say 'yes' to your wish, you must also say 'yes' to mine. We shall go to Sydney by the 'Agnes,' which sails in three days; and then, when my business is transacted, we'll go on to Auckland, pick up Miny, and bring her on here. Now, what do you say to my plan?"

"Just as you please, dear," she replied, leaning her head upon my shoulder, but not with her old loving trust. Now it came there wearily, as if for rest and refuge; and that day it struck me with a sort of timid uncertainty, much as a sick child lies down upon a nurse's knee, knowing it will be put aside directly the mother is out of the room.

The next two days were occupied in making the necessary arrangements for our journey, which would occupy several months at the slow rate of travelling then in force, the mails being all carried in sailing vessels, whose speed, of course, depended upon that very fickle element the wind. The "Agnes" was a new, and reported to be a fast vessel. She had the reputation, too, of being one of the best conducted and most comfortable on the service, so I congratulated myself upon the prospect of a pleasant voyage and the hope of seeing Lucy begin to smile again.

Having several other letters to finish that night, I sat up much later than usual. At last, tired out and half asleep, I went to our bed-room. To my surprise Lucy was not there, nor had she been to bed at all. I went into one room after another in utter amazement, making all sorts of conjectures as to what had become of her. At last, I noticed that the entrance door was not fastened. A horrible suspicion sent the blood curdling to my heart. The change that had been working in her since the birth of our child, and even for some time previously, together with many events trivial at the moment, but rising like burning lights in this moment before me, almost paralysed my limbs. My brain whirled, my eyes seemed staring as if afraid to look around in case they met the horrible thing I had conjured up. Just then a slight breeze forced the unlatched door open. The full moon was beaming clear over the garden, fields, and bay. Scarcely knowing what I was doing, I made my way down to the little gate opening on the road, and stood irresolute. Then a hope struck me, and, like a madman, I ran to the churchyard, which lay about half a mile distant. There were not many graves then, and upon our baby's grave lay Lucy, cold and lifeless.

CHAPTER IX.

WEARY OF LIFE.

When I returned to consciousness I was lying on a sofa in my own house, and Johnson was talking in a whisper to the doctor, who stood in the window. For a few moments I lay staring at them, wondering what was the matter, my brain seemingly held as by a tight band.

Presently memory awoke with a pang so acute, that the cold drops came to my forehead, and a horrible fear that my senses were forsaking me made my heart throb wildly. Fortunately my strength was great; and though the struggle was almost greater, I had strength given me for the time of need.

Johnson came up to my side, followed by the doctor.

"You are all right again now," said the latter, with his finger on my pulse. "I'll drop in in the course of the evening, poor fellow! I was not surprised. She had been ailing long. May God comfort you." And he left me.

"Johnson, tell me what has happened," I cried; "my brain seems filled with horrors. What did I do! What happened to Lucy?"

But the only answer he gave was a deep sob, as he laid his face upon the back of the sofa. I sat still watching and trying to remember what I had done and seen. Then rising I went to Lucy's room, the curtains of the bed were closely drawn. I pulled them aside.

She lay there, her beautiful young face white as marble, the long dark eye-lashes resting upon her cheeks. I stood like one paralyzed, until a hand softly clasped mine, and drew me away. It was Mrs. Gray.

"Do not stay here, Martin. You came to me when the hand of death lay heavy on my heart; let me comfort you now, poor boy. This is your first trial, perhaps. Come and talk to me. I will tell you all you want to know."

So she led me back to the dining-room, which was empty, and placing herself on the sofa by my side, told me what had happened. Some one had seen me run into the churchyard, and out of curiosity followed.

They found me fainting beside the body of my wife; and thinking we both were dead, went for help to the nearest house, which happened to be that in which Johnson was lodging. He managed the rest. The doctor on seeing Lucy said, she must have been dead more than an hour when I found her. He was prepared for this, he said to them.

The horrible suspicion that had at first entered my mind was fading away, when I felt a sudden impulse to search her room. So telling Mrs. Gray I should return shortly, and forcing her to let me go alone, I went to the bedroom.

I took up a case in which she kept her medicines, &c. It was nearly full, having been prepared for our journey. One bottle was gone, the laudanum, and that I knew had been brought home full that very day. Desperately, and almost like a madman, I turned over everything, hoping against hope that I might find it somewhere, but in vain. Then I ran down stairs, hunted through every box and closet in the rooms, followed by Mrs. Gray with a scared inquiring look on her pale face.

Fortunately she had no idea what I was searching for, and desisted interrupting me, from the belief I was delirious. I was still searching when the doctor returned. I questioned him closely, and, I believe, much to his surprise as to the cause of her death. It was no relief to me to hear she had been suffering from a complaint in her heart, dating from the shock of her father and sister's death, but aggravated by her confinement, a complaint he had warned her might at any moment cause her death; *I* thought only of the missing poison.

At last the doctor left. I then hastened

off to Johnson, determined to cross-question him as to whether he noticed anything to give weight to my suspicions. He was half lying on the table when I entered his room. Looking up quickly, he said, in a fiercely reproachful whisper—

" You have found it out. God forgive us! Why should she weary of life?"

" Then it is true. I dared not believe it, and yet I could not but do so!"

" Sit down, Tobin," and he spoke sadly, pityingly, " the bottle was in her hand. The doctor never saw it; what need of his knowing? Thank God I could save her memory from that reproach."

For a long time we were both silent. At last he spoke.

" Martin, I have much to tell you. You must know, and can bear it best now. I loved your wife dearly, before I knew she was engaged to marry you. She loved me then; but you came, and after she was your wife she loved you the best. God bless her —she was as pure and innocent as an angel. I was a villain; for I tried to win or keep her love, even after she was your wife; but she never suspected me. I told her of your meeting with the Millards, and she was never the same to me after that. Though she treated me as a friend in public, she was colder than ice in private; and roused me at last, until I almost hated you because she loved you. When that affray took place in the Hutt, in which you and Trevor had such an escape, a rumour got afloat that you had been saved by a woman who had once been your mistress. I never found out who started it; so do not question me: let me tell my story. But certain it is every one heard it, your wife among others. When you went off to the Otaki lately, the devil gained an advantage over me again, and I got her told you had been summoned away by the same woman, and then I asked her if she knew why you had gone so suddenly, and when she said she did not, volunteered to tell her. But she stopped me telling me she did not wish to hear the nature of any business you did not think it necessary to tell her of yourself. Believe me, Martin, I would willingly have given my life to unsay all that was said. That was the last time I spoke to her alone."

It is needless to dwell upon the sad days that followed. It was not till after her funeral that I ventured to look for any letter she might probably have written if the deed was premeditated. I found nothing except her diary, in which, though there was nothing definite, I could trace the gradual change. There were passionate expressions of affection constantly recurring, and with wildly uttered fears that she could not love me sufficiently, that she was not enough, and that if I had married another I should have been a happier man.

Sometimes too there were quotations from the Scriptures, and prayers for strength for herself, and the power to keep me from temptation. Now that the whole mystery of her sadness and anxiety in these latter days was explained, how sadly and reproachfully they came before me. Shattered and almost broken-hearted I could not force myself to apply to business. The world seemed a wide waste, life a burthen. I was alone and friendless, for I wilfully turned from all sympathy, and shutting myself up refused to see or be seen. The doctor tried hard to keep me up, giving out that I was suffering from a severe illness, as an excuse for my non-appearance, and coming himself daily to endeavour to talk me into reason, urging me to leave Wellington for a time, and take no rest, mental or bodily, until I had learnt to control and guide my own heart.

It was in vain he pointed out the wrong, folly, and even wickedness, of which I was guilty in thus warring against the workings and will of the Divine Power. The thought that I had been blind to my darling's real state was driving me to madness.

One day when the doctor came in, he informed me that Governor Fitzroy had arrived in Wellington, and was holding a *levèe* at the Club-House. After telling me of the conflicting rumours as to his policy with regard to the natives, he advised me to get a personal introduction to the governor, and ask employment of some sort: but I could not take his advice. The time had not come yet: but at last, when one day he advised me to join the ship that was taking Governor Fitzroy to Nelson, I obeyed, though I believe almost mechanically.

When I was once more astir, and in the society of other men, my grief took a more wholesome and Christian form. My affection seemed even stronger and deeper than when I was hiding myself from the world, when the whole day was worn away in struggling to bring, not only her face, but every word and action to remembrance, and that too with a never satisfied and disconcerted longing. Now all came unbidden. The words and actions of others brought some similar one of hers before me, and with an almost startling vitality I could fancy I saw her face. She was never absent now—close by my side, in my inmost heart—unseen, unfelt to all else she was there; far nearer, and, oh! far dearer than life itself; and making life even dear, when I had the power of thinking and feeling thus.

CHAPTER X.

A VISIT TO AUCKLAND.

When the intelligence of Governor Fitzroy's appointment had first reached the Company's settlements—and it began to be whispered that he had been at one time well disposed towards them, besides being a friend of Captain Wakefield's—great hopes were entertained that under his administration the settlements would again begin to raise their heads, and commerce flourish. How unhappily their hopes were frustrated is well known; and Governor Fitzroy's short rule is still looked back to with contempt and reproach. His examination into the cause of the Wairoa massacre left the settlers boiling with indignation and anger, mingled with apprehensions as to the results of his ill-timed leniency, and the depressing effect the concessions he then made would have upon the emigrants' interests. Rauparaha openly laughed at the policy pursued, and called the Governor an old woman.

After visiting Nelson, I determined to take advantage of a passage to Auckland in the ship carrying the Governor. We reached Auckland in winter,—that is to say, in July. But so great is the difference of climate between north and south, that I, for one, fancied it was warmer in this Auckland mid-winter, than in the Wellington summer.

My first impression of Auckland was intense disappointment, and though after a closer acquaintance with the progress made, the feeling wore off slightly, I still saw with a feeling of vexation what wretched mismanagement there had been at work, and could not help thinking what might have been done had some competent person held the reins of government and understood the economy of public money. Captain Fitzroy was fond of pomp, and very proud of being "His Excellency," so there was a continual round of levees, official dinners, government balls, and as these things cannot be done for nothing money meant for improvements or public good went in public pomp.

The streets were still only streets by courtesy; a house here, another there, interspersed with piles of timber, ready for cutting up or embarcation. In front of the

Government-house there was a court in which an attempt made at paving had singularly failed, leaving so many holes that the footway was absolutely dangerous.

Stumps of the mighty giants of the primeval Kauri forest occupied prominent portions in the thoroughfare, and in a dark night looked so like policemen, that I saw a newly-arrived cockney, in a state of partial inebriety, politely asking one to show him his way to the boarding-house he had put up at, but finding he received no answer, he made up his mind he had been addressing a native, and the story goes, wrote home the next day to say the English had taught the Maoris to stand guard in the town at night as policemen.

I had determined to go directly to Dr. Millard's house, but on my arrival I changed my mind, and ascertaining that Dick Hyde's station was only a two hours' ride, I hired an old broken-knee'd beast, dignified with the name of a horse, and set off for Woodfield, by which name Dick's farm was known.

The road bespoke the state of the country more strongly than anything. For a short distance it was tolerably firm, and bordered by a raised foot-path, along which women and children were travelling, some with large baskets of vegetables to sell in the town, others with bundles of clothing, spades, or implements of all sorts taken home for farm use. I saw a great many natives, most of them decently clothed in European garments, and in some cases so like emigrants, that I had to look twice before I could discern the difference. When I got a few miles out of Auckland the nature of the road changed rapidly, and soon became a mere track, with here and there a covering of large roughly broken stones in front of a settler's dwelling. These houses were all well-built and substantial-looking places, most of them embowered in flowering shrubs, and echoing with the constant accompaniment of homes in New Zealand, the voices of children, of whose health and strength of lungs the hearer can have little doubt.

A traveller seemed rather an unusual sight, for whenever any of the children caught sight of me there was a rush to the road, and I should have stood a bad chance of reaching Woodfield that night had I stayed to answer a third of the questions put by the inquisitive young monkeys, who I suppose become precocious in proportion to their strength of limb.

As I advanced, the country began to look much wilder; the clearings were, some of them, in a very rough state, many being only partially opened, others still burning, and some with the heaps of decayed and dead branches still lying upon them. In happy contrast to this were the clean, well-railed farms and tidy buildings of the older immigrants.

The distant views were some of the most beautiful I had seen in the colony, the pale grey of the mid landscape melting away into a peculiar shade of rose-colour, only seen beneath a New Zealand sunset, while the shades in the forest, composed principally of Kauri trees, grew darker and more sombre every minute, forming a striking frame round the bright green young grass in the clearings, or red brick and tile of the farm-houses and buildings.

Having ascertained that I had still five miles to ride, and being warned of a moonless night, I persuaded my steed to attempt something like a gallop, but at the expense of everything like ease or comfort to myself, being in fear and trembling that every step would bring him on his nose.

I saw little more of the beauties of the landscape, having my eyes and attention busy enough in looking out for the footway, and endeavouring to avoid stumps, very big stones, or ditch-like ruts. The road had been running through a large clearing for about a mile, during which time the sun had disappeared. Twilight was fast giving way before the approach of night, when, to my annoyance, and, I must say, perplexity, a turn and dip in the road shewed me a long stretch of forest, into which the path ran as into the mouth of a tunnel.

"Pleasant," thought I, "for a stranger upon a stumbling mare. I suppose it'll end in camping out for the night." One good thing, however, was, my mare was not blind as well as lame, and as I always make a point of trusting more to an animal's sight at night than my own, I laid the bridle on her neck, loosened my feet from the stirrups, ready in case she came down, and plying the whip pretty freely, kept her going a-head. For a few minutes I managed, by dint of straining my eyes, to see her ears, then they vanished. I held up my hand, but except when almost touching my nose I could not see even that.

It was lucky for me that my mare saw better than I did. She seemed much more at home in the dark than in the light, and feeling this, I kept plying the whip pretty freely, until sundry stumbles betokened rougher ground, and I was turning over in my mind the prudence of pulling up, when I was, greeted by a loud shout immediately in front of me, followed almost at the same moment by a terrific shock, and I found myself rolling upon the ground listening to a volley of oaths and imprecations upon my devoted and certainly bruised carcase.

As soon as I could gather myself and my senses together—for I had come down by what is called a run, and the stars and stripes incidental to a knock on the head were still dancing merrily before my eyes—having, I say, gathered myself up, I began to listen to my unseen assailant. There was something familiar in the sound, and likewise in the manner of speech. I listened attentively.

"What the devil do you ride that way for, you cockney fool? Do you think New Zealanders have cats' eyes? *By Jove!* if I could see you I'd give you something to remember your ride by. And what brings such as you up here at all?"

There was no doubt it was Dick Hyde himself whom I had thus unexpectedly stumbled on and over, and finding I had the advantage of him, I determined to have some fun.

"Have you lost your tongue as well as your seat?" he roared again; "why the devil don't you answer a civil question?"

"Friend," I said, altering my voice as much as I could, "thou art strangely mistaken. Thou ridest like the whirlwind, and having overthrown, thou mockest thine adversary."

A loud laugh greeted me.

"Come, no chaff! There are no Quakers out here. Is it you, Bob Scott?—or you, Joe Temple? Come, enlighten my understanding, for, by Jove! unless I can find my fusee box, there's small hope of enlightening anything else."

"I am neither Robert or Joseph. My name is Benoni, the son of affliction. Thou art full of intoxicating liquor, Richard Hyde, or thou would'st not have ridden thus recklessly to thine own as well as a stranger's overthrow."

"By Jove!" I heard him exclaim under his breath; then aloud, "I know it's all chaff; but you're a sharper fellow than any I know about here, though unless you're the devil himself, I don't know how you've twigged my name. I was christened 'Richard,' I do believe; but I've been so long 'Dick,' that I'd well nigh forgotten the other. I wish to goodness you'd tell me who you are and where your horse is. I've got hold of mine, and we may as well ride on together."

"Be it so, friend Richard; but I must walk by thy side; the animal I bestrode has departed."

"Nay, then, catch hold of my leg and mount; mine will carry double," said Dick.

Nothing loth to get free of my precarious Rosinante, and glad of a chance to carry the joke a little further, I accepted his offer, and, guided by the voice, made my way to his side.

I could feel Dick's warm breath. Dick put his face close to mine, but it was no use, he could not see me. He then ran his hand over it—this was equally unsatisfactory; and with his favourite expletive of "By Jove!" he became silent, and we rode on.

I saw by the distant glimmer that we

were approaching another clearing, and that concealment would not be possible much longer.

"Where are you bound for?" said Dick, suddenly breaking silence.

"To thy house, Richard Hyde."

"Indeed! Perhaps you can tell me your business now; I could meditate upon it properly here."

"My business will wait, friend," I replied.

So we approached the open in silence. Once there, Dick's eyes were again in my face.

"By Jove!" he shouted, "Martin Tobin! You infernal rascal! why did you set up for a Quaker? What the deuce could put such an idea in your head? Why, you're but the ghost of yourself."

"Ah, Dick, old fellow! I've a deal to tell; let's wait till we get in."

Dick gripped my hand as hard as a vice for a second. He told me afterwards he knew then, as if by instinct, what I was going to tell him; so that when standing before a blazing fire I told him of Lucy's death he was not unprepared, but Dick was a warm and sympathizing friend, and his kindly words and comfort did me a world of good; he questioned me as to why I had come to Auckland, how long I had stayed, and many other things, especially if I had seen the Millards; and I fancied he seemed relieved when he heard I had come straight on and seen no one.

An old hag about seventy, answering to the name of Diana, brought in supper. After her portion of the duties had been performed we proceeded to do ours, and very effectually too, I assure the reader, I, for one, having come in verging upon starvation! but when Diana had carried off the last dish, Dick and I had drawn our chairs towards the fire, and filled our pipes, were prepared for a quiet evening. I felt all the comfort a friend's hearth and welcome can yield.

I told him more concisely than I could before my whole sad story; and he began to make plans for me, trying hard to persuade me to begin farming with him, giving me all sorts of proofs of his own prosperity and the prospect held out to any steady colonist.

Just then I did not know what I was going to do, or, indeed, whether I should remain in the colony at all. Daylight still found us smoking and talking, Dick explaining it by saying it was so long since he had talked to an idle man, that he could not let me go to bed in case I should begin to be as busy as every one else was when I woke.

He declared himself worked to death, and sick of the whole concern, only waiting to make out his five hundred pounds, and shake the dust off his feet against the colony for ever.

In spite, however, of his often repeated invectives against New Zealand, and his disgust at what he called the slaving life he led, and a whole string of grievances from want of decent company down to the impossibility of getting boots in Auckland,—in spite of all this I saw Dick was becoming a capital settler, that he had already collected no end of little comforts round him inside the house, and if the supper set before us all came from home produce, he had verily not let the grass grow under his feet; and it was with some curiosity I waited for the daylight, that I might see what he really had done.

CHAPTER XI.

MINY MILLARD'S NEW HOME.

DICK'S farm lay on each side of a pretty stream forming one of the tributaries to the *Karrarurae*. It was as yet only partly cleared, though the process was rapidly advancing, from the fact that he employed a large body of natives in clearing, paying them by the acre, after the example of some of the oldest and most prosperous settlers in the islands.

The fields immediately round the house

were all well inclosed, and in first rate order. The farm buildings were substantially built of a grey sort of stone found at hand, and costing nothing beyond the cutting and carting.

Dick had laid out a portion of his money in purchasing a few wild looking young horses and a small herd of cattle, so that with the constant accompaniment to a New Zealand farmer, a flock of sheep, he had his ground amply stocked, and found plenty of work to do.

In spite of the really good opinion I had long ago formed of Dick, I was astonished, and I believe, slightly envious of his success as I walked round his farm, and listened with no small surprise to his dissertation upon the prospects of growing this, or breeding that. I had always fancied there was a good foundation of strong sense and energy under the crust of frivolity; but I confess I was not prepared for the excessive change I now saw.

"You're surprised, Martin," he said, as we sat smoking in the verandah after one of the pleasantest days I had passed for a long while. "Well! I'm not, for to tell you the truth, I had no notion of what a settler's life was. I'm not apt to be humble; but I didn't think I had it in me. You see they were right at home. I was made for an emigrant. I think they'll open their eyes at home when they find out what I've done. I'll send my brother a cheque for five hundred pounds next month if the markets keep up. You saw that young mare to-day, in the field next the last clearing, I was offered seventy-five pounds for her the other day, and her brother went off to the colonel at the barracks for one hundred pounds. I've three as good, fit for the breaker now, and there is a young bull I expect fifty pounds for, after he takes the prize at the autumn show. Upon my word, Martin, you're kinder to your friends than yourself. Here you are, very little richer than the day you landed, and here am I, an idle good-for-nothing dog, coining money on the loan you gave me. You should take ground, old fellow. Hard work deadens the heart-ache better than ought else. When hard thoughts come up I get to work, they generally give way before it. Come and take the next claim; the owner wants to go south, and will part with it for next to nothing."

"Would he take an exchange?"

"Where?"

"On the Wanganui."

"To be sure he would, the very place he's taken up with. If your dinner's digested, we'll ride over, and see how the ground lies. Nothing like doing things at once. Believe me, Martin, I've gained by following this up; just think for a moment, and you'll believe me."

So in a few minutes we adjourned to the stable, and after saddling our horses, cantered off on our way to the farm spoken of, though, as Dick said, the next clearing lay fully six miles off, and through a close forest track.

At first we could canter along at a pretty good pace, but presently the path grew rougher, and at last suddenly dipped down into a steep dark ravine, from which rose the rumbling din of a waterfall, and the rank oppressive smell of decaying vegetation.

"Give him his head," shouted Dick, keeping up his pace, and getting on before me; "he knows every inch of the way."

So I trusted to his advice, and though prepared any minute to find myself spinning through the air, managed to look about me, and take in a few of the external and natural beauties of the glen, or pass; for such it was, being a wide and deep cleft between two considerable hills, completely curtained in by gigantic trees, and festoons of the *aki*, &c., whose deep red blossoms hung like bunches of coral over head. The damp and mossy soil beneath, teemed with ferns, moss and lichens, making every yard of the road or path a perfect study. As we made our way up the bank on the opposite side, Dick let me get alongside, and beguiled the last two miles by an elaborate description of a diabolical outrage committed by some convicts in that very dell, the ring-leader rejoicing in the name of "Black;" but whether the same I knew, I of course could only guess, though from the description given Dick by the native who told him, there had been no doubt in his mind.

"I suppose you know Black has taken to the natives," observed Dick in an off-hand way.

"No, I've been trying to trace him for the last two years, and could not manage anything. What do you mean by taking to the natives?"

"Well, that's easily explained, fraternizing with them. Black made even this state of society too hot to hold him. A reward was offered for his apprehension, and half-a-dozen of his old comrades had taken an oath to win it. So he accepted an asylum in that rascal Rauparaha's pah, got himself tattooed, and passes off for a native, they say, so that he has deceived some of the Maories themselves."

Here was a disclosure and explanation of many things. I questioned Dick closely, and without giving him a hint of my experience, knowing how apt he was to embellish if he got interested.

Clari's presence, fear, and death, were all accounted for now, I had actually been in the presence of the man I had searched for far and wide, and not only in his presence, but may be clasping his hand, eating off the same dish, and sitting looking into his face for hours, without the slightest suspicion of the truth. When I had heard all I could from Dick, I told him of my having been in Rauparaha's pah, and my suspicions that Black must be the man who went by the name of Kauri. This he could not give any opinion of, but as it was important, and in the event of the war, (now muttering in the distance), breaking out, and might be very useful knowledge, we determined to keep the suspicion secret until the fitting time came, following them up if any opportunity offered.

Dick's acquaintance had changed his mind about migrating to the south, giving a very good reason in the unsettled state of things, but he promised to give me the refusal of his place, which (though in a bad and slovenly state, the result, not of want of money, but want of industry), seemed good wholesome land, capable of great improvement, possessing the advantage of first rate outbuildings, and a couple of hundred acres of splendid Kauri forest, sloping up the breast of a pretty hill, and as it lay further down the river than Woodfield, it had the great advantage of water carriage.

A vast number of natives seemed congregated about this place; nor did I altogether like their looks. And even though assured by both Dick and his friend, that they were perfectly harmless, and ready to take up arms any day for the sake of the settlers, I thought they looked as if they would much sooner take them up against the intruders, a supposition, time unfortunately soon proved too correct.

Instead of riding off home, Dick proposed we should pay another visit. I reminded him of the want of moonlight, but he said he knew the road perfectly; besides, we might possibly be able to find a bed, in which case we could return by day-light.

So we cantered on along a road very similar to what we had traversed in the morning, but soon breaking into a wide table-land, covered with fern, only broken in spots by clumps of trees.

Dick's miles were evidently Irish; for after a two hours' ride, when I ventured to suggest a proposal that something in the way of bodily refreshment would not come amiss, and that possibly the next party of timber cutters we came upon, might be induced to satisfy the cravings of appetite, he very coolly informed me, that we had better canter on, as we had only an hour before sunset, and nearly eight miles to get over, and some rougher ground than we had yet come. There was no use looking reproachful. Dick's back was towards me, and as for words, I knew of old, he did not care much for them. Distance in a new colony is little thought of; but I must say this was a little unreasonable.

"Don't think it far, do you?" exclaimed Dick looking over his shoulder.

"Oh! dear no, a mere trifle; only thirty miles, I imagine."

"Don't be impertinent. You can't make a joke, old fellow. You never were up to it. The distance is close upon twenty miles; but then you see, I have taken a a holiday on your account, and want to shew you the country—lionize a bit you know. You don't express your gratification?"

"I'm confoundedly hungry, that's the

fact; and would give something handsome for a bottle of something moist; I'm past caring what."

"Well, we'll try the next lot of fellows logging we come across. They generally have a black liquid they call rum."

So we rode on at a sharp enough pace when the state of the track permitted. Still there was no appearance of any living being, much less clearing, and my parched lips refused to articulate my disappointment, while Dick, who seemed invulnerable to either compassion or feeling, whistled, sang, and talked, without a moment's intermission, and until my patience was pretty nearly exhausted, and I was on the point of pulling up and insisting upon trying to find a spring to quench my thirst, when he uttered a loud "*Coo-eh,*" and putting his horse into a gallop. I followed. A turn of the road brought us to the edge of the forest, on coming into the light of heaven again, I saw stretched out before me a beautiful and wide valley. The bright blue ocean lay on one side, belted by a broad white beach; on the other, by high mountains looking almost indigo colour, against the golden flood of sunset.

At first I had seen only the larger characteristics; now I turned to the others, and to my intense surprise, observed a scattered, but good-sized town, flourishing farms, and at the next turn a large and well filled harbour. I pulled up and stared.

"Where in the name of fortune have you brought me to, Dick?"

"Oh! you don't give us northerners half credit enough. You think you've concentrated all the energy in the south; but you see what we can do. Now you'll be able to enlighten your friends' understandings a little. Come, push on my boy; you'll get something to drink, without much trouble here. We'll just see if we can wash the dust down at the 'public;' then go and make our bow before dark."

Another mile and a half lay past neat houses and gardens, gradually assuming the character of a street, coming in at dusk to a more formidable looking building with a sign-board informing the public that beer, cider, and spirits were to be had in abundance, we gave our horses to a lad, and turned into the bar, where a lively young lady, whose complexion and black eyes denoted native blood attended; with this lady Dick was evidently on good terms, as she invited him into a back room, where we found a jolly old gentleman, whom

Dick called the Major. After a short conversation entirely confined to the state of the clearings, and news from England, we walked off to make the call which I mentally voted must be very delightful, if it repaid such a journey.

A walk of five minutes brought us to the gate of a snug villa, surrounded by a well-filled garden, with English as well as tropical flowers. Taking a side path, we approached the house. The door stood open, and Dick, without any ceremony, walked in, and rapped at a door. Getting no answer, he ushered me into a pretty little drawing-room, opening to a conservatory. A few water-colour drawings hung upon the walls; work and an open piano betrayed a woman's presence, and a half-finished crayon sketch likeness of Dick himself, began to give me a hint of his anxiety to make the call, and oblivious as to the distance between his home and the object of his admiration.

Seating myself upon a rocking-chair, I was balancing comfortably and cogitating as to the fun I should get out of Dick for his cunning, when the door opened and he entered, leading a lady, who curtsied gravely. It was Miny Millard. There was no doubt of it; no mistaking the pleasant kind face and sweet earnest voice.

"I suppose I may dispense with the ceremony of introduction," laughed Dick. "I am very sorry, Miss Millard, that Mr. Tobin had such a long ride; he must feel the exertion."

"Come now, Dick," I exclaimed, "you did not tell me whom the call was to be upon. I had no notion the doctor had left Auckland."

"Nor has he," answered Miny. "Mr. Hyde cannot do anything like other people. He has only taken you a round of I do not know how many miles, to bring you here and win a laugh."

And as I turned to say some thing to Master Dick, he was taking his departure from the room.

CHAPTER XII.

DICK'S CONFESSION.

HAVING obtained an insight into the timidity of the Governor's character, the natives became impressed with a very exalted idea of their own importance, and by way of proving to us what they could do if it pleased them, determined to give a great display, fondly imagining that having once seen them in the power and war points, the settlers would be cautious, and by succumbing to native power, save the colony from bloodshed.

The feasts and gathering were to come off, under pretext of hospitality to the Governor; and accordingly a great number assembled, gathering from all parts, the armed warriors amounting to fifteen hundred.

This meeting took place upon the fern plain I had crossed during my first ride from Auckland to Woodfield, and here they feasted, danced, made speeches, boo-boo-ed at each other and the Governor for several days, parading the streets of Auckland, and purchasing whatever they could in the way of clothing. Having impressed the settlers with a proper knowledge of their strength, they dispersed as quietly as they had collected.

The reader may imagine the effect such a

display had upon a handful of peaceful and almost unarmed men. The soldiers were as nothing in comparison to the multitude of active and ferocious Maories, in most cases only a degree removed from the savage and cannibal, while those professing Christianity and civilization were if possible still more formidable enemies.

The meeting had a still wider and more pernicious effect than merely alarming the settlers round Auckland. For as many of the natives had come from distant parts of the island, they carried home a highly-coloured description of their proceedings, laughing openly at the fear displayed by the Governor, numbering the English by the trunks of the trees, and their own tribes by the leaves.

Another evil, which though scarcely felt in the first instance, had led in a great measure to the subsequent discontent and bloodshed, was this: the natives who had lived in the country, and apart from the settlers, now for the first time saw and understood the wealth and comforts possessed by the settlers, and these they at once attributed to their prosperity in New Zealand; arguing, that if they had been as rich and happy in their own country, they would not have exposed themselves to all the dangers and trials of such a long journey. If the strangers, therefore, were able to get such beautiful things out of the ground, why should not the Maori? They knew the way now, and it would be very easy to drive out the settlers, and take possession of the tools and means used by them.

Before the monster meeting at Auckland, there had been a somewhat better feeling stealing among the southern tribes. Te

Heu Heu was our chosen friend; and as Te Whero Whero's possessions and his formed two of the boundaries of Rauparaha's, that chief dare not risk any open display, though taking advantage of every difficulty to "*boo boo*" or bounce at the English.

Mr. Spain, who had been chosen to arbitrate the land disputes, was at this time deep in the Company's claim at Taranaki, and his decision was to be deemed to be final. Before it was given the influence of the "Monster Meeting" had reached Taranaki.

Many natives, who had formerly kept friends with the English through fear, began to grow insolent, and walk about carrying arms of all kinds, helping themselves to whatever they fancied. Mr. Spain saw the storm brewing, and sent off a special messenger to Auckland to give notice of it.

In the meantime a native row, ending in a hardly contested fight had taken place above Kaipara, near the mouth of the Wanganui. Some of the fugitives took refuge with Rauparaha, carrying intelligence of the affair with them. To add to this Honi Heki threw out hints that were not to be mistaken.

The horizon was clouding in from every point. The Governor, driven to his wit's end, set off for Taranaki, by way of conciliating the natives, and, as he said, averting bloodshed, he set aside Mr. Spain's verdict, ignored Te Whero-Whero's claim, wronged and offended the Company's settlers past all retribution, and lighted the train which was to end in the war which is still rankling in the colony.

On Governor Fitzroy's return to Auckland intelligence of a new danger reached him.

The decay of the whale fisheries and timber trade had affected the prosperity not only of the English, but the natives also, at and near Korrorariki.

The natives could not understand why the ships did not come as formerly. At last a rumour rose that England was at war with America, and that the American vessels dare not come; so Heki decided that if the English were driven out, the traders would come again; and accordingly assembled his forces, attacked Korrorariki, cut down the flagstaff, and marched back to Haikone in triumph, leaving the inhabitants of the town in a state of considerable alarm.

Dispatches to Australia, demanding reinforcements, left the same day that the intelligence reached the seat of government; nor was this uncalled for, the detachment of the regiment then in barracks, only numbering something like a hundred men.

The interval that must elapse before the reinforcement could arrive was one of anxiety and continual alarm. And though the settlers were very desirous of forming a militia, the Governor set his face against it, as likely to excite the natives still further. The whole community was filled with indignation, numberless letters were written home, representing the true state of affairs, beseeching those who could to put the true account before the country, and endeavour to have Governor Fitzroy superseded.

Dick Hyde grew quite energetic, and was on the point of starting with the mail, the better to bring about the desired climax by personal evidence, when news of the arrival of troops in the Bay of Islands turned his attention to what would be the next move.

Either Dick or I rode daily into Auckland to inquire for news; and when it became known that the Governor had offered peace, had accepted a dozen old muskets as damages for the insult, and had declared Korrorariki a free port, it was with difficulty the settlers could be kept quiet, and only by the conviction that they had no power to supersede the Governor, but must wait with what patience they could for orders from England. Dick brought this news home to me one night, and at the same time announced his determination to get up a volunteer company, setting the Governor at defiance. I highly approved of his plan, but had made up my mind to cross to Korrorariki.

I had been some months at Woodfield, and every few days had thrown me into Miny's society. At first I had endeavoured to avoid her, from a sort of fear lest I should revive my old attachment, but I soon found my love to poor Lucy was a shield against any other. Miny was a dear friend, but no wish for a nearer tie ever entered my mind. Indeed I saw with regret that she gave no encouragement to Dick's honest and openly expressed admiration, and that the poor fellow, in spite of his utmost endeavours to hide it, really becoming jealous of my presence.

The day I announced my intention to volunteer my services, and cross to join the troops, Dick had been in Auckland, and, as usual, doing his best to win a smile of approval from Miny. A deep flush coloured his face, when I told him of my determination. I saw, or fancied I saw, what he was thinking of.

"Would you mind telling me exactly why you are going, Martin, I asked."

"Not a bit, man. I've nothing to do; and I think an idle man's a nuisance among a busy lot."

"But haven't you some other reason?"

"None that I know of, except it be a wish to be in the thick of danger. I'm tired of the world, Dick, that's the truth. I never knew how I loved poor Lucy till she was gone; and now I don't care how soon I follow her. That's the truth."

"Then you don't want to marry Miny Millard?"

"No, Dick; I think Miny's a dear good girl, and would make any man—you, for instance, if you could win her—a first-rate wife."

"Thank you, old fellow. She wouldn't take such a stupid brute as me."

"Try."

"I have tried; aye, tried with all my heart. Why, what do you suppose made me keep steady here? Not love of farming, you may be pretty sure. No, nor love of the colony neither, but love for Miny Millard. You don't know how I've learnt to love—no, love's no word for it—to worship that girl. I think it began the first day I saw her; long before I knew you, or heard your name. I've never seen any girls like her — so natural and kind, without throwing herself at your head like some, or making love to you just for fun, like others. No, she is just like a man, but a thousand times better. She will hear you talk of things you cared for, and give you advice. She will ride or walk alone with you without thinking you were going to make her an offer. Every word she utters is—"

He stopped abruptly, and looked hard at me.

"You're not laughing at me?"

"No, no, on my honour, Dick; but it is so queer to hear you getting into heroics upon the tender passion."

"You don't doubt my sincerity, Martin, old boy?" he asked, with such earnestness that I thought I saw something like moisture in his eyes.

"I'd as soon doubt my own senses, Dick. God bless you, old fellow, you've my best wishes. Miny's worth any man's work. Don't give up. You'll starve out the garrison in time; she's half won already."

"No, though! do you mean what you say? I thought she was awfully cold the other day—until—I mean—but it's no use mincing matters; I have been jealous of you, Martin, and had half a mind to tell you, you had no business to be hanging about her until I began to think you were going to offer. Then——"

"Well, what then?"

"Oh! nothing. I'd have paid you your money, and gone back to old England, I suppose."

"And since I'm not going to fall in love, but wish you every success, what will you do?"

"Well, I hardly know; what would you advise? Go on, as I am at present? pay off my debts, get the money from home, and set up a country gentleman out here? I wouldn't care to stay if Miny wouldn't have me."

"Try her first."

"No, I cannot. She would say 'no' just now. I see it in her eyes. She's not got over her—"

"Hold, there, Dick! I don't want to quarrel with *you*, of all people; so don't let anything of that kind come between us. Most of us have a secret chamber, or, as some call it, skeleton, somewhere. Our best and dearest friends cannot meddle with it. They had best know nothing of it—or, if they must know, they are *wisest to ignore it carefully*. Let the past be the past, Dick. You found out by chance what you would never have heard from me, and need never have known anything of. Let it be forgotten. I cannot afford to let it come between us, and unless we understand each other now it will do so."

Dick clasped my hand.

"Then you do wish me success, and don't think Miny still cares for—"

"There, you're breaking ground already.

Miny is the same to me as a sister. She thinks no more of me than she would of a brother. And when I come back from the wars I don't mind taking long odds that I shall find you and her engaged, or next door to it. Now let's have a tumbler of grog, and to bed. I'm off to-morrow."

And so I was. For, having made inquiry during the week, I had ascertained a small sloop was to sail for the Bay of Islands; and, although I had not taken any passage, I knew money would get me that, at any time or hour.

So many changes had taken place since I visited Korrorariki before, and were moreover all crowded into such a short period of time, that it was difficult to realize that the interval was anything more tangible than the delusion of a dream.

The journey had been marked by nothing

particular. We crossed H. M's. ship "Hazard" on the way, but it was blowing fresh at the time, and we could not do anything else than answer the signal for news of the expected mail, by a negative. On reaching Korrorariki we found the soldiers had all left for Auckland, the Governor having accepted Neni Walker's offer to garrison the place, and thus left the settlers at the discretion of the natives.

Disappointed and angry with myself for being in such a hurry, I took up my quarters at an hotel kept by an old naval purser, who divided his time between drinking rum and spinning yarns about the battle of "Trafalgar."

Before many days had passed I was thoroughly content with myself for having come, feeling convinced that what was past was merely the muttering of the storm that was gathering over this portion of the colony, and that a few weeks at most must see it burst forth. News came in daily of new and more insulting acts committed by Heki and his adherents. In spite of the new feature of a free port, very few vessels made their appearance, and as the Government officers could not get money to pay for the keeping up of the public works, the improvements were stopped, and many able-bodied men thrown idle upon the town.

Neni Walker took everything with the greatest coolness, contenting himself with what the niggers call "talkee-talkee," and, as far as I could judge, though willing to receive the praise of the English, and be considered their friend, was equally unwilling to come to open blows with his countrymen.

At this juncture, and about a week after my arrival Heki marched up to a pah close to

Korroráriki, where his warriors had been of late now daily paraded, insulting the settlers with perfect impunity, and utterly disregarded by our allies, who prudently, perhaps, at all events, carefully kept within a certain district, avoiding all collision with the others. The settlers and storekeepers were in a state of the greatest mental anxiety; some of them, having been dealing pretty largely on Government credit, were on their last legs, and had too good reason for upbraiding the Governor as likely to be the ruin of the whole country.

For some time after my arrival at the Bay I had found plenty to occupy my leisure in the town itself, consequently had not gratified my curiosity in visiting the position taken by Neni Walker, though from what I heard I was very anxious to see it, and only waited an opportunity for its gratification. At last, finding I had a vacant day, I set off to pay our great ally a visit. Few at the time sufficiently appreciated the value of this chief's adherence to our cause, and friendship to us as a people, and consequently he did not receive the respect or consideration which it was not only our duty, but our interest to pay. I found his pah in a state of complete defence, his warriors mounting guard, and sentries posted in imitation of the English garrison; and had I not been accompanied by a townsman and storekeeper well known to the natives, I should not have been admitted. As it was there was no small fuss, demur and questioning, and half-a-dozen well-armed natives conducted me to the presence of the great man.

I found Neni Walker a frank, intelligent fellow, ready to praise the settlers, and give them the credit of raising the character and prospects of the country, but exceedingly careful what he said regarding his own people. Heki he evidently feared and hated cordially. Gossip said they had a private grudge regarding Heki's wife, who was not very exact in her conduct, and had at one time shown no small favour towards Neni. Be that as it may—and Maori gossip is pretty similar to European with regard to truth—it was plain there was secret provocation. And Neni's cheeks grew flushed, and his eyes sparkled when he mentioned Heki's name. With great hospitality he insisted upon my remaining all that night, assigning an empty hut for my sole use, and offering to call it mine, so that I should have an inducement to come and visit him often. After supper, prayers, and a pipe, he conducted me to the hut, looked round to see that I had everything comfortable, then shook hands, and wished me a good night's rest.

I found an oil lamp burning beside my bed, and a Bible, with Neni's name written on the first page. As I opened it, my eyes fell upon the words "Say to them that are of a fearful heart, 'Be strong, fear not.'" I had read them last with Loo, and they now appeared to speak to me from her grave, and I was bending over the words of comfort when the sound of many voices struck my ear. I listened, and heard the Evening Hymn sung by some hundred voices, the well-known air thrilled through my heart, rising as it did in the stillness of night, and in a far off land, where, until the last few years, the very name of Jehovah had been unknown.

With a feeling of indescribable awe, I stood up, and taking off my cap, listened with a full heart to the sweet sound. Suddenly it was hushed, and a powerful and almost supernaturally clear voice broke the silence, and repeated the words of the Lord's prayer, followed by a blessing; then all was still, and I sat down again to read, with a new strength and my heart echoing the words, "Go ye into all the world and preach the gospel to every creature."

Following up the thoughts awakened by the voice of praise, and words I had just been reading, I again lost sight of any outward sound, and looked up with a start and exclamation of surprise as a light touch was laid upon my shoulder, and the voice I had just been listening to deepened by the accents of prayer, uttered my name. I looked up, and saw an Englishman, evidently from his dress a missionary, bending over me. There was something in the face and eyes that carried me back in thought to my boyhood and Slyndhurst; yet I did not recognize him.

"You don't remember me, Martin?" my visitor said, with a sad smile, his hand still resting on my shoulder. "I must be more changed than I thought. Cannot you see a single feature that will bring me back to your remembrance?"

I snatched up the lamp and held it close to his face. I knew him then, but my heart shrank back. I remembered only my wrongs and his deceit; they rose like a dark wall between us. The holy words I had been reading fled from my heart, giving place to a very rage for revenge; and if ever the devil was by me in spirit tempting me to my eternal destruction, it was at that moment, when, with my hand half raised, I was on the point of striking him; suddenly Lucy's voice seemed to ring in my ears, and repeat the words she had used when I told her of all Frank Cary had done: "Forgive him, Martin; he did not know he was making me the happiest woman on God's earth." My hand fell, and covering my face, "I wept bitterly."

CHAPTER XIII.

TIME WORKS WONDERS.

NEXT morning Frank told me his story. He had come out as chaplain on board an emigrant ship, bound only for Sydney; and after staying in Australia for some little time, partly that he might learn the Maori tongue from an old missionary he fell in with, and who offered to teach him, partly to get acquainted with the different localities likely to suit the men in charge of whom he had gone out, he took passage in a ship bringing reinforcements to the Bay of Islands; and finding Neni Walker anxious to get a missionary teacher into his pah, had there located himself.

No wonder I had not recognised him. At first I could scarcely trace a resemblance to what I had seen him in days gone by even when I knew who he was. Life had been no matter of repose or ease to him; and the deep furrows of study and pain were stamped indelibly upon his face, while his hair prematurely streaked with grey, had grown thin and hung carelessly over his forehead.

A life of dissipation and excess at college had brought on a severe illness; for months his life hung upon a thread; and even when strength of constitution overcame his bodily ailment, his brain still wavered, and nearly a year elapsed before he recovered. A great change had been wrought in him during his illness; he had been placed under the care of a clergyman who had been very many years a missionary, and who, finding that Frank in his more lucid moments would listen attentively to him while he described the exciting and deeply interesting adventures he had experienced in his good work amongst new and almost unknown lands searched out and read the most stirring descriptions he could meet with given by other labourers in the Lord's wide vineyard.

The result was, that Frank's return to sense and reason was like awaking from a long dream, the events of which were clear upon his memory. But more than this, he seemed to have passed through a second period of childhood, and his character becoming pliable as at first, received and by God's blessing retained the new direction thus given. And much to his friend the clergyman's surprise and joy, he became aware that unconsciously his work of kindness had made Frank a new man.

As soon as able Frank applied to the Emigration Company for the appointment which had brought him out to New Zealand. That part of his story which related to Miny seemed the darkest spot upon his memory. Bitterly, indeed, had he repented, but though repentance is a balm and relief, it does not remove the remembrance of pain and agony that has been. It was with a sort of determination to sacrifice every personal feeling and hope by finding me and explaining his share in the deceit that had been one of the principal motives in bringing him to the colony. But how dear Miny still was, became too evident in the emotion he showed when I told him all that had happened.

Though his quivering lips betrayed the pain he suffered, he questioned me step by step as I went, asking over and over what Miny said, how she felt towards Hyde, and then what I thought she might learn to feel. Suddenly as I was speaking he laid his head upon the table, and groaned heavily. "Oh, Martin!" he said, "I would to God I'd never seen you again, or been tempted to come here." Then raising his eyes to heaven, he repeated the words of that beautiful hymn—

"I thought that I was strong, Lord,
And did not need thine arm,
Though troubles thronged around me,
My heart felt no alarm.

I thought that I was rich, Lord,
That all good things were mine,
And earth and all its pleasures
Did my vain heart entwine.

But thou hast broke the spell, Lord,
And roused me from my dream;
The light has wak'd my soul, Lord,
With bright unerring beam.

I know that I am weak, Lord,
That nothing is my own;
But thou wilt make me strong, Lord,
Leaning on thee alone.

* * * * *

My soul in death was sleeping,
But thou hast given it life;
And strengthen'd by thy Spirit,
I'm ready for the strife."

Poor Frank! I could not feel any enmity towards him as I saw him now; I had seen more changes even than he had, and, strange to say, our boyish days and affection seemed to be revived again; so that when the grey dawn broke in upon our watch, we had opened our hearts to each other as of old; and I lay down to take a hasty sleep, a happier man than I'd been for many a day.

Frank I do not think even attempted to sleep, for when I closed my eyes I saw him kneeling, and when I opened them he was pacing the hut, a bright colour in his cheeks, and that unmistakable gleam in the eyes that tells so surely an anxious, restless spirit.

Soon after daybreak, the whole tribe assembled for prayers, Frank reading and explaining a few verses in their own language; and as he spoke of the sin and sorrow, passions and angry thoughts brought upon the human race, I saw more than one man shed tears.

Meeting with Frank had given a new direction to my wishes and plans; I became his constant companion, and while doing so, saw more of the real habits and character of the native race than I had yet had an opportunity of doing. And every new insight I obtained tended to confirm the opinion first hinted to me by Trevor, namely, that mismanagement of the government and ignorance, combined with indiscriminate enthusiasm of the missionary body, had poisoned and warped natures which in their primitive state were capable of receiving an impression of the very highest degree of morality and civilization.

As it was, the natives, as a body, were deceitful, avaricious, and time-serving, ready to take any advantage they could of the settlers, and eager to obtain money and luxuries at any price.

When the news reached us that the British Parliament would not acknowledge the treaty of Waitangi, the consternation already existing increased a thousand fold, especially among the nativès. Heki sent letters and private messages to all the chiefs, telling them that if the treaty was not held good they would lose all their lands and be made slaves and servants. Mobs collected and harangued each other in all directions, and finally we in the town, left helpless by the absence of authority, were obliged to look on idly while Heki marched up with a couple of hundred men, and again cut down the disputed flag-staff, Neni Walker contenting himself with advising him not to do it.

The first result was the arrival of detachments from Auckland, bringing with them a small body of volunteers. The 96th Regiment re-erected the flag-staff, surrounding it with a stockade, left a handful of men to protect it in case of an unexpected attack.

No sooner was the flag again floating over the devoted city, than a proclamation from Heki became the topic of the day. He stated, that "seeing the English considered the flag as a token that the land was theirs, he would not permit it to remain." Every one knew he would keep his word; and there was not a man or boy who did not volunteer to learn something of military exercise. This went on for some weeks, until in March Heki advanced up close to the outskirts of the town. The first I heard of this was on meeting an officer of the "Hazard," who told me a boat belonging to her had been fired on, and one of the lieutenants taken prisoner.

There was something very like a panic in the town when this became known;

and though nothing further was done, and the captured lieutenant was sent back unharmed, we all recognized the spirit of the chief, and his cunning in not rushing to extremities. He gave us fair warning, and by acting with such hypocritical leniency towards the first captive secured the good-will and offices of the missionary bodies, who, at that time, as in the present day, sacrificed the settlers' interest to a romantic idea of keeping up the Maories as a separate people—an attempt which, I cannot help thinking, is against both the laws and precedents of Scripture history, and completely at variance with what we know to be the precedent in profane history.

The Sunday after this act of warning, or, as some of the people called it, Heki's challenge, Frank proposed to me to accompany him to the enemies' camp, as he intended to make an effort to convince them of their folly, in attempting to fight against the English. Although I had no hopes of his succeeding to the extent his more enthusiastic nature anticipated, and very little of his obtaining even an entrance and hearing, I readily consented to go with him, partly out of anxiety on his account, partly from curiosity to see the great patriot—for such I must confess I considered Heki—in the stronghold he himself had chosen. Some hours before daybreak we went forth upon our mission. The walk was not a long one, but being across a ridge of hills, occupied some time. Frank was almost perfectly silent, evidently too deeply impressed by the importance and solemnity of what he was risking, and what he might accomplish, to pay attention to any of the lesser events of the hour, and when I drew his attention to the magnificent sight that burst upon us, as we gained the high ground on the mountain, and looked back upon the bay bathed in the golden rays of sunrise, while the air was filled with what the early navigators beautifully compared to a chaunt,—the morning praise of myriads of little bell-birds,—his countenance lighted up with a glow, such as might beam on that of a martyr, as he felt the last chords of life giving way, and his freed spirit already stretching her wings to bear him beyond the agony and weakness of his earthly trial.

"Who could look upon such a scene and doubt that God has formed it for peace and happiness," he said fervently. "Look at it, Martin, drink in to your inmost soul the silent, as well as the uttered praise. God made them all for the joy of man. 'Behold I have given you every herb bearing seed, which is upon the face of all the earth, and every tree in which is the fruit of a tree yielding seed, to you it shall be for meat, and to every beast of the earth, and to every fowl of the air, and to everything that creepeth upon the earth, wherein is life, I have given every green herb for meat. And it was so. And God saw everything that he had made, and behold it was very good.'

"O, Lord, what shall we render unto thee, for all thy goodness; or how shall we thank thee enough for thy mercy in restoring to us the happy prospect of a sinless and eternal participation in a world made by Thee, and undefiled as Eden, when Thou first pronouncedst it "very good." And then, with a voice, trembling with emotion, repeated:—

"His praise, ye winds, that from four quarters blow,
Breathe soft or loud, and wave your tops, ye pines
With every plant, in sign of worship wave.
Fountains, and ye that warble, as ye flow,
Melodious murmurs, warbling tune his praise;
Join voices all ye living souls, ye birds
That singing up to heaven-gate ascend,
Bear on your wings and in your notes his praise.
Ye that in waters glide, and ye that walk
The earth with stately tread or lowly creep
Witness if I be silent morn or eve,
To hill or valley, fountain or fresh shade,
Made vocal by my song, and taught his praise!
Hail, universal Lord! be bounteous still
To give us only good, and if the night
Have gathered ought of evil or conceal'd,
Disperse it, as now light dispels the dark."

"Ah! Martin you feel it too. I seem to drink in a sort of inspiration, as I gaze upon the glorious works of the Almighty, unsullied by the hand of man.

My very soul seems throbbing to break its bonds, and soar away from this prison, fair though it be. And yet it is sinful to feel thus, and weary of the road He leads me along. Yet I do weary, Martin, and long with an inexpressible longing for the end."

"When will it be, Frank?" I said, after a pause. "I mean, when do you think the great end of this mortal frame will come?"

"Not long, friend; not long I firmly believe," he replied; "the voices are growing louder every year, nay, I may say, every month. The signs are thickening around us, and though the roll of his chariot-wheels has often seemed to come, and then died away, the night is almost past, the dawn is near—nearer, perhaps, than either of us thinks." Then, after a short silence, he said, "Do you often think of these things, Martin?"

"Not so often as I ought, Frank, but oftener than I did before Lucy taught me. She never said much; but somehow everything about her seemed to have anchored in heaven."

"You never told me of her death, friend; did she know that she was dying?"

The cold drops sprang to my forehead, the words hung for a moment on my lips. I did not know I had uttered them, but they must have reached his ears.

"Good God! poor thing!" he muttered; then added, "forgive me, Martin, I had no idea of this. Do not speak of it more, now, but to-night, when we return to the town, you shall tell me all. I see you do not want comfort from earth, for you have it from heaven. I can understand now why you do not feel it possible to entertain mortal love again. You have passed a terrible ordeal. Thank God, you have not lost faith in his inscrutable justice; and can wait for the explanation of those mysterious ways, which to us are as darkness."

As we drew near the fortified position taken up by Heki, we saw the English flag waving triumphantly over the stockade. It was the same flag he had taken, in his first expedition, and hoisted in token of victory. Presently a shrill whistle, close by us, was answered from various points, and a native sprang from behind a bush, and presented a musket at Frank, he being a little in advance. For this, however, we were prepared, having ascertained the password for the day from one of the native teachers, who had indeed assured us that Heki would be friendly, and had often expressed a wish to have the Church service performed regularly, even when in arms. The man lowered his gun, and we passed on, repeating the same scene several times, until we reached the breast-work; then a native followed us, and having ascertained what Frank was going to do, and that he was Neni Walker's missionary, he seemed very much pleased and shouted to each person he saw, the news that a missionary had come to pray and sing; and before we reached the spot, where the huts or barracks were erected, a great many natives followed us, and others were running up from all directions.

Heki was sitting beside his wife, when we were introduced into his apartment, and though of course quite aware that we were coming, from the minute we had entered the pah, he affected great surprise, pretending to be very angry at our daring to come without first asking his permission; and then, after making a long speech, about the cunning, impudence, &c. of the English and their many bad acts, contrasted with the morality and holiness of the converted Maoris, he ordered Frank to proceed to a place prepared for worship, and, turning to the people round, bade them pay attention to the good words, and show the stranger, meaning me, a good example.

Frank preached in Maori, choosing the text, "Whence come wars and fightings?" During the time he was speaking there was a deep and impressive silence, and I could see many of the natives quivering with surpressed emotion and excitement, which burst out as soon as the sermon was over, and seemed to annoy Heki, who, though by no means a correct Christian, in spite of having been brought up by the missionaries, was a great stickler for forms and ceremonies; and was wise in his generation too, for by keeping up the semblance of Christianity, and using far-fetched similes and very inappropriate texts in his proclamations and letters, he deceived a great many persons, and obtained among a certain class a character for piety he by no means deserved.

I think he must have been ashamed of his friends that day; for he had evidently lost command of his temper, when he came towards Frank; and, after thanking him, in a very ungracious manner, for his sermon, ended by recommending him to go and repeat it to the English, for that they were the cause of all the evils of war. Then, without having the courtesy to bid us farewell, he walked off to his quarters, leaving Frank and myself in the midst of an excited and noisy mob, all eager to ask questions, and few able to restrain their impatience long enough to wait for the answer, even had an answer been always possible.

Frank knew enough of the native character to perceive that, in all probability, the present dispute would end in a fight, if the exciting cause was not removed; so shaking hands with one or two of the most friendly of them, we took our departure, not sorry to have escaped without more trouble. I could see that Frank was deeply disappointed, though he struggled hard and unceasingly to find excuses for them, blaming himself as the cause, and regretting, though most unjustly, that he had gone, in preference to inducing some more eloquent man to undertake the duty.

CHAPTER XIII.

A HUNDRED POUNDS FOR A GOVERNOR'S HEAD.

A FEW days after this Heki marched to the top of the hill and again cut down the obnoxious flag. Neni Walker mustered his warriors and talked big, but did nothing more; and though there were numbers of the settlers ready and well-armed, the flag was down before they knew of it; and what could they do against such overwhelming numbers as swarmed up the hill and through every street of the town?

There seemed no end to them, and, drunk with what they considered their great triumph, insulted the settlers on all sides. Next morning several of the natives walked through the town, proclaiming a reward of a hundred pounds for the Governor's head, causing much laughter among the settlers, many of whom, to tell the truth, would have been by no means very sorry to hear the reward had been claimed, as the events just now taking place were the fruits of his weak policy, and every day seemed to increase the irritation against him.

There was nothing to be done but to recall the detachments, a most unfortunate movement and it was the third time that this had taken place. Heki retired, but on hearing that the flag was again erected, this time surrounded by a stockade and guarded, he made his appearance on the neighbouring heights, surprised and took the position, drove back Captain Robertson of the "Hazard" who with a handful of sailors, only retired, when literally out of breath from fighting, and when they saw retaining their post was utterly hopeless.

I was in Neni's pah when the firing gave the first alarm, and at once suspecting that the threatened attack had again taken place, I urged Neni to come forward in defence of the rights he had promised to protect inviolate. He quite agreed with me, and made a great fuss about calling his warriors, and forming them after the fashion of an English regiment. Disgusted with his hypocrisy and cowardice, I called to the warriors to follow me, but not a man stirred.

When I reached the path leading up

to the barracks I met a whole crowd of terrified women and children; and heard that the flag was cut down, and that the soldiers were coming back. The loud boom of the big guns belonging to H. M.'s ship "Hazard," now gave forth tokens of real war. The whole town was panic-struck, the population came crowding on to the beach, and hurrying, with scared faces, into the boats. The terror and confusion was presently increased by the explosion of the powder magazine, and all hope of restraining, or making any sort of stand against the savages completely put an end to; and soldiers, men, women, and children were shipped off on board the vessels lying in the bay. Once there, and in safety, they began to collect their senses. The hill presented a strange sight; it was covered with natives, whom we afterwards heard, sat down to watch the townsfolk running away, utterly bewildered at such an unexpected proceeding, and attributing it to the power of their war-god. Their amazement soon found vent in great rejoicings, and with telescopes we could distinguish them haranguing, and frantically dancing war dances, before they took possession of the deserted town.

As soon as it was daylight next morning, I went on shore; and landing about a mile to the left of the usual harbour, walked direct to Neni Walker's pah, with the intention of upbraiding him for his conduct. I found the great man in a bad humour. He had sent to see what Heki intended to do with the plunder of the town, demanding—though upon what grounds I scarcely knew saving that he had not opposed—a share of the same. And upon

Heki sending him back a scornful refusal, he put on his war-paint, and seizing his musket, made a long and brave speech to his people, during which he took so much exercise, running up and down and gesticulating, that being an old man, he regularly broke down, and was obliged to stop talking from sheer inability to proceed. I had come in for the latter part of his speech, and certainly if words could have annihilated Heki, the war would have been at an end. And perhaps had the old chief's strength not given way at this critical moment, he might have done something to retrieve his character; for he was very eloquent, and had worked up both himself and his warriors to the pitch of excitement; howls and yells resounded through the pah, muskets were flourished about as their owners sprang frantically in the air, and countenances, hideous enough already with tattoo, and hastily daubed war-paint, were distorted until perfectly diabolical.

All this was at its height when the orator suddenly paused, and after making a painful effort to continue, sat meekly down. Had a shock of paralysis seized the whole pah, it could not have effected a more general hush, or arrested the wild gestures of the excited listeners more completely. There they stood, some with their muskets uplifted, others with the horrible grimace still on their faces, but every eye fixed on the chief, whose mysterious silence they at first attributed to a supernatural cause. Then gradually as the truth became apparent, and they knew that weakness and old age had conquered their great leader, they slunk away with downcast and sorrowful countenances to mourn over their disgrace.

Frank, ever ready to seize a moment that appeared favourable to make and leave an impression, stood up, calling upon them aloud to stop. A few did so, and after he had addressed them for a while a number returned, but so sadly, and with shame so plainly written in their faces, from which they hastily wiped the war-paint, that I could not but feel touched, particularly when I noticed that not one of them looked at Neni, who still reclined upon the mats where he had fallen, keeping his face buried in his blanket.

When Frank had finished speaking, Neni Walker rose, and although I could see every one was straining each nerve, and the sob of their suppressed breathings throbbed through the throng, not an eye was raised from the earth. Solemnly and with proud dignity and sadness I never saw equalled, Neni spoke. At first he spoke in a cold measured tone, relating the old story of the first peopling of the country; then going on to describe the coming of the English ships, and how friendly he had always been to them. So far his speech seemed to cause little excitement; but at this portion he threw off the calm exterior he had chosen as a veil at first, and burst forth with a torrent of reproaches, comparing himself to a pine, which though it may have lost its sap and may not spread forth new branches, stands firm as a rock in its place, sheltering hundreds of younger trees beneath its mighty arms.

Strongly impressed by his eloquence, and wondering what reception it met with from his people, I turned from the excited and flushing face of the speaker. A visible change was working in the crowd. Now and then a head would start up, or an indescribable sort of movement, almost like a pulsation, thrill through their closely drawn ranks. At last, as if simultaneously, every head was raised, and hundreds of fierce passionate eyes flashed their answer.

He continued speaking for some time longer, and told them that he intended following Heki to his pah, and there demanding reparation for the insult he had given to the friends of the country; that having failed in his attempt to keep the god of war out of the land, the sin was now not his to answer for, but Heki's. Then turning to Frank, he held out his hand saying,

"Heki has despised my words, and thrown my speech back in my teeth. He has taken hold of the muzzle of the gun, but I will take the stock. I have said to the west wind bring peace, and to the true God of the heaven, give us hearts to love each other; but I perceive that my thoughts are not His thoughts, and that we are as the dust of the earth before the breath of the Great King. Go, tell the Governor whom your Queen has given us, that he can send soldiers to help me with their manner of fighting. Behold! I and my warriors are ready."

Heki having gained only one day in advance upon his journey to his old fortification of Oheawai, Neni followed him foot by foot, establishing himself within a few miles of the spot chosen by Heki as his final halting place; and it was eventually through

Neni that we received such constant information of the enemy's movements.

Instead of returning to their old habitations, the fear-stricken settlers insisted upon being conveyed round to Auckland, which, from its proximity to Te Whero-Whero's domains, and his known friendship towards the English, they were confident would escape any attack. Volunteer corps were formed, and taking up a position near the barracks, the settlers made good use of their time in learning military drill.

When the reinforcement reached us we had by no means a despicable company to join them, and formed, with a few additional men who came from Auckland, ninety-five or a hundred strong, making up the force, independent of our native allies, to about four hundred, the whole under the command of Colonel Hulme. Oheawia was to be the point of attack, some of the troops going by sea in H. M's. ship "Hazard," the rest making forced marches by land, following the track left by the enemy and our ally.

Being no soldier, and ignorant as to military tactics, I dare not give an opinion upon the system pursued in sending men a long and difficult walk, when they could so easily have been transported by the more comfortable and less fatiguing route by sea; though from the fact that I shared in the hardships, exposure, and real privations of the journey, I might, perhaps, be able to offer an opinion worthy of attention. Be that as it may, the plain facts were unfortunately evident. The men arrived near the pah, worn out and dispirited, exhausted from want of food, and though in good health, in great bodily discomfort from the state of their clothing. For, having no practice in erecting any sort of shelter, and, being unable to carry tents with them, they were forced to sleep in the open air, under the droppings from trees, and on the wet ground. Thus their uniforms became hard and wet, chafing their limbs, and in some instances bringing on boils and sores. Besides this, May in New Zealand corresponds to November in England, and it scarcely ceased raining during the four days' march.

The pah against which our force was to march lay on the shore of the lake. It was strongly fortified, and when we arrived there were several working parties busily engaged in what were no bad imitation of trenches. Soon after we had fixed upon our position a deserter from the enemy was brought in; and from him we learned that a reinforcement of eighty men had just joined Heki from Rauparaha's country, led by no less a person than Kauri himself. The intelligence, important as it was in regard to the additional force, only possessed one feature in my eyes—the fact that Black was there, and that the chances of the fight might bring me into a life and death struggle with him.

Soon after dusk the natives in the enemy's pah commenced singing hymns, and continued so doing the whole night. The effect upon our men was very painful, either exciting them to irreverence, or awakening a superstitious fear and uncertainty as to the justice of our cause; so that, combined with the sufferings on the march, they were in rather an unsatisfactory condition.

Upon the eighth an attack was proposed, planned, and about to be executed, when a messenger from Neni reached the Colonel, explaining the nature of the native fortifications, and the utter impossibility of storming the pah in the manner proposed. So Colonel Hulme had to content himself with advancing three storming parties up to the verge of the outworks, and firing half-a-dozen rockets into it by way of surprising and intimidating the natives. While this was going another native from the enemy's pah was brought in, who, in great fear of immediate decapitation, informed us that an ambush was laid, and offered to show us the way.

Though doubtful as to the accuracy, the Colonel deemed it prudent to make sure, and sent a party of the 58th and marines to reconnoitre, and these falling in with the ambush as stated, after a slight skirmish, drove the natives back at the point of the bayonet inside the fence of the pah.

After surveying the position from every point, and finding it must be breached by large guns, the troops retired upon Overoa, leaving many gallant fellows cold beneath the green sod, and the reflection rankling in the breasts of their comrades, that the advance had been as ill-timed as weak and objectless. Colonel Hulme carried the wounded off to Auckland, leaving the rest in garrison under the command of the Major of the 59th.

I heard from Dick Hyde, who was present on the return of the Colonel, that his reception was a very doubtful one. Nor did I feel any surprise that it was so. For a few weeks only had elapsed since he left the capital in command of a fine body of gallant men, who, with a proper guide, could have brought three times the number opposed to them to terms, whereas the only news they brought was of disappointment, if not absolute repulse, together with the unwelcome fact that the enemy were daily increasing in numbers, and raising new fortifications. To the settlers better acquainted with the temper of the natives the events had a much more important signification. The prospects of the colony wore a threatening aspect, growing darker every day.

At this juncture the Governor seemed to rouse from his lethargy, and begin to comprehend the true position and peril in which he stood. He organized another expedition, and saw to the arrangements personally. The landing took place at the Overoa, on the mouth of the Kari-Kari river, just about a month after our inglorious and ill-judged retreat—a month which had done the work of years on the impressible natures of the Maoris, increasing, not only their numbers by the arrival of allies from many of the discontented pahs in the south, but giving them too good cause to sneer at the policy of the English as people who liked, they said, to *bark* without caring to *bite*.

Colonel Despard, the new commandant, had now nearly seven hundred men under his command, assisted by four large guns, the men of H. M's. ship "Hazard," and two hundred and fifty of the native allies. Neni was expected to join us, but was cut off and defeated by Heki before reaching the troops.

Upon the 23rd of June we started on our advance on the pah, no one doubting that we should carry all before us, and almost laughing at the notion of such a large force being brought out against a wooden stockade, and a few hundred undisciplined and naked savages. How terribly we underrated their power, cunning or courage, whichever you may call it, was shortly and too fatally evident.

CHAPTER XIV.

STORMING THE PAH.

The pah or fort of Oheawai stood on a large plain surrounded on all sides by the forest. Great pains had been taken to render it as strong as possible, and at the same time to disguise its true strength, so as if possible to tempt a charge, thus giving proof that Heki was not slow in learning a lesson in strategy. We commenced hostilities on the 24th of June, by firing the big guns. These made little impression, owing, I suppose, to the peculiarly elastic nature of the breastwork and stockade erected by the natives, which, being entirely constructed of whole trees freshly cut down, seemed actually to close up after a shot, while the natives themselves were all hid in holes hollowed out beneath their huts. The firing was continued until the first of July, when Colonel Despard, growing weary of such desultory work, and confident in the power of disciplined troops over the untrained warriors, decided that the breach effected was practicable.

A storming party was told off, consisting of a hundred and sixty soldiers, and forty sailors and volunteers, among the latter your humble servant; for although I must confess to having no particular wish to attempt to carry the pah at such very great odds against us, the thought that I might come in contact with Black was sufficient to spur me on. There was a solemn pause of some five or ten minutes after the storming party was formed, and then for the first time I felt my heart throbbing with eager excitement. I looked round on the faces of my men, and saw the same written in every countenance. The advance rung out clear and hopeful, and with an involuntary cheer on we rushed. For a few minutes everything seemed a dream. Then I found myself struggling with a half-dressed native, my sword gone, and no weapon but a broken musket. As we rolled over clasped in the embrace of deadly strife, I caught a closer sight of the man's face. It was Black, or Kauri, as he was called now. I had time to recognise him, when I felt a sharp sting in my breast, and my arms becoming powerless, he sprang up. The thought that I was killed flashed across me. I tried to rise, but fell back. Just then with a bitter imprecation and shouting Black's real name, a sailor bounded past me, and grappled with him. I saw no more. A strange sickening sensation stole over me, my brain swam, and I remembered nothing until I returned to consciousness several hours after, and found one of the surgeons standing beside me, and heard we had been repulsed. Frank was near me kneeling beside a poor young fellow who had been shot in the back, and was dying.

In a few words the surgeon told me the sad story. We had lost about a hundred men, among them William Grant, of the 58th, and Philpott, of H.M.'s ship Hazard, both gallant fellows, and beloved by their comrades. Both fell in advance of their men, happily killed on the spot. One poor fellow, a sailor, who from the description I gave of the man whom I had seen fighting with Black must have been the same, was known to have been taken prisoner. Frank, to whom I related this, went off to make some inquiry, and presently returned with the information that I was perfectly correct, but then came a fact that affected me deeply, namely, that the sailor was a man Philpott had picked when in one of the southern ports, that he had formerly belonged to the service, but had ran off and been living amongst a tribe on the middle island for several years. Thus, strange to say, I came upon poor Tom and our mutual enemy on the same day about the same moment.

As night gathered in, the scene became solemn and painful. Fires were lighted, round which litters were .laid with the wounded, while a short distance off a guard stood round three bodies of those who had died from their wounds since the attack.

Soon after dark the natives inside the pah began to sing and beat drums, occasionally firing a volley. Then, after this prelude of some ten minutes, a deep silence ensued, producing a strange effect upon our men, who seemed to hold their breaths and wait for some coming evil, many of them saying afterwards that they felt their flesh creep with an indefinite horror, while others stood up with their muskets cocked, fully persuaded there was going to be an assault. In the midst of this a prolonged shriek that made every heart thrill with horror rose from the middle of the pah, and was repeated three times at intervals; then a voice which was recognised now as that of poor Tom, shrieked in accents of terrible agony—

"Oh, my God! they're skinning me alive," every man heard as if personally addressed, and mad with horror, thirsting for revenge upon the cowards who could thus torment a defenceless man; it was almost impossible to keep the men back, and the Colonel had difficulty in preventing them rushing promiscuously to take vengeance and attempt to rescue the prisoner. This excitement grew greater still as it somehow became known that Kauri was in the enemy's pah. Again and again during that awful night did the dark forest echo with Tom's cries of agony, though the words "Oh, my God!" were now the only words he uttered. The grey dawn was just breaking when Frank, who had been sitting by my side, his face buried in his hands, suddenly rose up, exclaiming—

"I cannot stand it, Martin; I must try to help the poor fellow. God bless you! if I fail, and do not come back to tell you so, think kindly of me, and——but no—God bless you!"

One clasp of the hand and he was gone. An hour after his body was brought in pierced by half-a-dozen bullets. He was quite dead, and death had come instantaneously and without pain. His features were fixed and calm, with a placid, sweet expression written on them, that looked almost like the reflection of a smile. When his death became known Neni Walker's men flocked round, many of them sobbing and shedding tears over the marble-like face which lay there up-turned to heaven.

My wound was bad enough to oblige me to take passage with the wounded men to Auckland, where, truth to tell, I was by no means sorry to be again, the night after the repulse having effectually sickened me of savage warfare.

Of Tom we heard and could hear nothing, except that he was still alive. I have no doubt that his having met with Black had led to the severity of his punishment. And my only regret in being obliged to leave at that period was the uncertainty I felt as to his fate. Had I remained I could have done nothing towards his relief; still, it was with a painful feeling I saw the shores fading away. Poor young Beattie of the 99th had died a few hours before we started; and this, added to the peril in which we could not but acknowledge our men were placed, surrounded by natives, many of whom only waited for an excuse to turn upon us, and throw off the mask of friendship they found it so difficult to keep on, kept us anxious enough.

A few days after our departure, and directly a fresh supply of ammunition reached them, Colonel Despard began firing again, and kept it up until a Maori came into the camp and told them the pah was empty, a favourite dodge, as it seemed. At first, his information was looked upon as only a weak attempt to entrap the English into an ambush, but after a time it became evident that the case was as he represented; and on examination it was found that Haki had actually retired secretly in the night and taken up a position at Ikorangi, about ten or twelve miles off. Here Heki erected the famous pah, the model of which has created so much surprise, and which seemed to hint at an acquaintance with the rules and principles of fortifications, far beyond anything ever before executed by so called savages.

On my arrival at Auckland the first news I heard was, that the governor had sent orders to Colonel Despard to move down to Korrorarika and take up his quarters there until the enemy made an offer of peace. At first none of us would believe that any man in his senses would be guilty of such a suicidal policy, but on landing it was corroborated, and equally condemned on all sides.

No answer had as yet been received to the despatches praying the English Parliament to look into the affairs touching colonial interests, or to provide more adequately for the government of the colony, than by sending out a man to hold the reins who knew nothing whatsoever of the people either in temper or character, and who only cared for the appointment on account of the title it gave him.

The first person who came on board was Dick Hyde, and I fancied his honest face looked something graver as unseen by him I lay and watched him questioning one of the men about the movements of the troops, and listening with contracted brow to the detail. At last, thinking it cruel to let him be in suspense. I holloed out his name. He was instantly at my side, full of pity, kindness and anxiety; for the despatches had given an account of Frank's death, and Dick had been drawing upon his imagination for the truth. Miny had heard, too, and been very much shocked; and though she said little of me or my doings, he was sure she brooded over them, and grew paler and sadder as day after day went by, and not a message or line came from me. It was in vain the doctor told her "no news in this instance must be good news," as if I were dead, or anything fresh had happened, my name would be announced in the lists published in the newspaper office. She could not rest, and had that morning begged Dick to cross the country, and look after me himself, a proceeding poor faithful Dick was actually going to put in force, when he heard that a ship with the wounded was in sight.

So after running back to the villa to beg the doctor not to tell Miny, in case of raising her hopes to be again cast down, he came off to the ship. But whether, finding me rapidly becoming convalescent, and returning in such an interesting light as a wounded man only fit for nursing was not a subject of some regret, I will not vouch. Verily, it would be against human nature, and I thought none the worse of my friend though it was so.

Nor could I marvel, for something almost akin to my old love began to knock at my heart as I looked into Miny's glistening eyes, and read there more than she knew herself, and enough to make me decide upon going out to Woodfield the instant I dare undertake the journey, and thus carry myself away from the dangerous proximity of an old love, and the chance of some old root throwing forth a fresh shoot.

CHAPTER XV.

MINY RELENTS AT LAST.

In spite of my wish to leave Auckland, I was unable to do so for several weeks. The heat of summer setting in just on my return, brought on a degree of inflammation about the wound that prostrated me; and, contrary to my usual health, I seemed to sink down utterly powerless.

The doctor and Miny were kind and wise nurses, and Dick stole about the room with such a solemn quiet face, that I often felt a nervous desire to break forth into a loud laugh as I lay and watched him.

Poor fellow, he was on the rack day and night, I could see that; and soon had proof positive one evening, when I was just able to crawl into another room, and dose idly on the couch.

I was lying half awake and half asleep, when Miny stole softly into the room, and thinking I was really asleep, sat down with some needle-work, forming such a pretty picture that I did not care to do more than lie and contemplate it. Suddenly she looked towards the garden, and a deadly pallor spread over her face, followed by a deep flush. She rose and threw aside her work, as if to leave the room; then with a suppressed exclamation of annoyance sat down again. At the same instant I heard a step in the hall, the door was opened, and Dick Hyde came in treading as gently as if on hot iron. He crossed over to Miny, and sat down upon an ottoman near her. She had picked up her sewing, and was stitching away diligently, as it soon became evident, much to Mr. Hyde's vexation, for in a whisper I heard him say, with a very poor attempt at a smile,

"Are you working against time, Miss Millard?"

There was not much in the question, so from the flush it brought to Miny's cheek, I inferred there had been some passage of arms previously, a conjecture proved correct by her answer.

"I thought I had said enough this morning, Mr. Hyde, and it would have been wiser and better for us both, if you had gone home for a few days; you said it yourself, and——"

"Oh! Miny, I could not. I got half way across the plain, and then something came over me, and for the life of me I could not do it. If I had gone on I should have cut my throat when I got home, upon my soul I believe I should."

Miny laughed a forced, threatening laugh, that always shews a woman feels insulted.

"You might, perhaps, have endured your own society, if you had tried and spared me."

"Miss Millard you are angry," he said, "and no wonder. I am a regular fool to come here again, after all the kind advice you gave me this morning, and I've no right to be telling you what I feel or think. But you would pity me if you knew all I have suffered since poor Martin came back."

"How dare you now"— Miny sprang up with her lips and eyes quivering. He seized her hand.

"Sit down, Miny; it was to dare that I came back. Hear me out; I must tell you sometime; if not now, to-morrow; if not then the next day. We have our fates, I suppose—mine is come."

So Miny could only sit down to listen; and as both seemed to have forgotten my presence, I still lay as a spectator. Dick pleaded his cause eloquently and from the heart. He told how long he had loved her, and described his agony and jealousy when I returned; and then—I almost repented of listening—what I had told him of never wishing to love again. This was evidently the part he had come back after his first dismissal to tell her. Miny heard it coldly, and without outward sign.

"Then you do not love him, Miny?" he asked, bending over her and trying to catch her eye.

She was silent for an instant, then, pointing to a seat, said in a low, cold voice,

"You have been candid with me, Mr. Hyde, and your past friendship deserves some requital. If you will listen I will tell you what I never told before, or dared even to think of and acknowledge to my own heart. When Martin did not write to me I did not doubt him, but found excuses, until I could frame no more; and then the opportunity occurring, I urged papa to come here. You are aware that I found him married. I found too that he had written, and had heard sufficient to convince him that I was either married or engaged to another. I suppose men are more easily shaken in their trust than we are. Possibly they see more of the falseness and blacker side of life. At all events he was married. I tried to love his wife, who was very kind to me; but I could not; and, in spite of myself, I was growing morose and reckless, when my father accepted this appointment, and brought me (I did not come willingly) here. I seldom heard from Wellington; but some one wrote and told papa of his wife's death. You will believe me, Mr. Hyde, when I tell you, I felt her death more deeply than the fact that she was his wife. From that moment I have hoped he would go to England—anywhere so that we never should meet again. But he came here—and—I know he does not and never will love me. You hinted that he knew I loved him. If he ever speaks of it to you, tell him that

I do love him, but the very love with which my whole life has been filled would forbid my being his wife. I shall remain as I am, Mr. Hyde, and when you can come to me and bid me be your sister or friend, I shall be content and happy. Till then, remember every reflection, sad enough already, will be more deeply darkened, and the life that is a burden seem harder to bear."

"God bless you, Miny!" sobbed Dick, with her hand in his; "and God will bless you, for you tell a fellow the truth. I'll never tease you again, and when I come back, you need not be ashamed to take my hand and tell me all your troubles. God bless you for ever!"

Miny sank back in the chair, as he closed the door, and for a few minutes, I feared she had fainted, so perfectly motionless was every feature. Then a torrent of tears burst forth and she rushed from the room, leaving me in a very unenviable state. And though, in thus playing eaves' dropper, I had not heard any evil of myself, I had heard a great deal more than I wished of myself, and was heartily sorry I had done so.

I lay nervously debating as to what I ought or could do, and was heartily glad when the children came in to tell me Miny had a head-ache and was not coming down again; but hoped I would let Kate pour out my tea, and take care of me.

The reader may understand me, when I say that I was in a dilemma. I lay awake all night turning it over, only to come to no better dccision, and when I got into the sitting-room lay dreading to see and speak to Miny, so alarming the doctor by my irritability; and I could see he was in no small degree relieved when a message came to call him away.

Miny did not make her appearance, till past mid-day, and then affected to be so busy with household matters, that she only stayed a minute to inquire how I had slept, a proceeding which no doubt kept her mind at rest, though it began to agitate and disturb mine.

At last I decided to move off to Woodfield next day in spite of bodily weakness,—a strong proof I now think of great mental debility. I told Miny I was going, and she quietly acquiesced, looked even relieved, especially when she heard her father assure me if I felt equal to the journey, I should benefit by change. Poor old man! he had grown weary of the restraint my presence proved, and in spite of the affection I knew he felt for me, was not sorry when he found I was determined to risk the journey.

Next day having been provided with an impromptu palanquin borne by natives, I departed, Miny's pale face being the last I saw as I looked back from the gate.

My arrival at Woodfield created quite a sensation. I had made great friends with the solitary, or—I believe the technical name is—sole-servant, besides getting on good terms with the workmen and their families, and as soon as my approach was announced, they all sallied forth to meet me, honouring me with quite a little ovation.

Dick was not at home, having gone off to a distant station to buy grain. So I turned into my old quarters, and being pretty well knocked up, went to bed leaving a pencil note on the table explaining how I had taken advantage of his absence to locate myself. I was roused out of a sound sleep by Dick's joyful "hollo," and was obliged to sit up and help him to get through supper, a meal seldom to be sneered at in New Zealand, where men are too busy to waste time over a daylight meal, and must wait for the night to indulge their gormandizing propensities.

From the care with which Dick avoided all reference to Miny, I could see how painful the subject was, and said not a word. So time rolled on. The lull that had taken place in the late storm of words and weapons seemed to affect even the private dispositions of the people, and there was a pretty general feeling of relief, but this did not last long, rumours of war began to float about again, and while the whole colony were breathlessly looking for what was coming, Governor Fitzroy received despatches from the home government, politely informing him that his exertions though highly appreciated, &c., &c., &c.—in short that he had been superseded by Captain George Grey, a man whose prudence, foresight, and tact had been amply proved during his governorship in South Australia, the vicinity of his appointment and experience in the character of the Polynesian races equally pointed him out as the fittest man to take in hand the arduous task of fixing British authority in New Zealand. Never did any one undertake a more difficult or delicate task; one which he fulfilled conscientiously, giving himself up heart and soul to his work, and winning the affection and respect of both settlers and aborigines.

And now seeing every prospect of an interval, at least, of peace, and having made rapid strides towards regaining my old state of bodily energy, I determined to take an expedition in search of Tom, of whose death I had heard nothing; and still in my own mind I felt convinced that he was alive.

"Shall I go with you?" asked Dick, when I announced my determination.

"Not unless you wish it."

He made no answer, but, by the clouds that curled up from his lips, I could see he was debating as to the answer. Presently he dashed his pipe on the ground exclaiming,

"Then if you won't take me, I'm off to the diggings."

I stared.

"Are you mad, Dick Hyde? You off

to the diggings! What do you want with such things? You are coining money here quite fast enough to be respectable. Why it would be like flying in the face of Providence to leave such a farm as this."

"I can let it. Dixon of the Peak would give his ears for it. He told me it would be worth five hundred a year to him.

"And you pocketed five hundred the first year. What would he do with the clearings?"

"Just as I do. He taught me that."

"Then you've been thinking of this before; how long?"

"Since I came up from Auckland last."

"Oh!"

"It's all her doing, but now I think of it you were in the room. I saw you just as I got out of it."

"Yes, Dick, and confoundedly sorry I was too. But what can I do?—I came off after you. I've no wish to spoil your peace of mind, old fellow; and if you take my advice, you'll stick to your work here, and persevere in the other quarter. Leave time to take up your cause."

"No, no, Martin, I've made up my mind to leave this place. In fact, the bargain's clinched. I could not get off if I would. The rent is five hundred per annum, paid in advance. The first goes home to-morrow, so I may say I'm independent of the farm. The price of the stock will reach something like a thousand—quite enough to keep me for a cruize even after paying your loan, and then hey! for California!"

I saw remonstrance would come too late, and so held my tongue, waiting to hear what he had been determining upon, before I asked him to go with me to the south.

"I was wondering whether I should go with you first, Martin," he began, "but I think not. I might get a hankering to come back just for a last look, you know, for life ain't certain at best, and hangs on a hair trigger, among the diggers, they say. If you're unlucky you're in the way; and if you're lucky you're put out of it, to make way for others. Still, I'd like to see the sort of life, I should have no time for moping there; and upon my word I should be turning sentimental if I stayed here much longer. Only last night as I was riding home from the Peak I caught myself gazing at the moon, and wondering whether Miny ever looked at it. So you see what I'm likely to turn to if I idle on here in this jog-trot sort of life. I didn't think that way of it till now, you'll say. No, I didn't; but then mind ye, I had something to jog on towards. And however slow the trot was, I fancied, at least I hoped I was getting nearer the goal. You know how this ended, and I don't care for the pace now."

"Perhaps I may join you, Dick," I said; "I don't seem to care to stay here, though I believe there's not a better country under the sun. Still, since these rows with the natives came on, I can't say I altogether relish it. I should like to go to sleep without being afraid of finding my ricks on fire, or perhaps a musket ball travelling through my flesh; flesh and bone don't cut up so pleasantly I know from experience. I'm a peaceful man I suppose, so unless things take a turn under our new Governor, I'll cut the concern, and go back to England."

"I don't expect you will, Martin, you'll

change your mind. and small blame if you do. She's not happy."

"There you are out, Dick. If I thought there was any chance of my changing, it would be all the stronger reason to clear off in time. There's no use putting an imaginary wall before you. You'll succeed yet, Dick, or I'm a bad prophet."

"Never! Martin."

"You'll try, old boy."

"I said I would not."

"You didn't say you would forget her."

"No."

"Will you ride down with me to-morrow, when I go to say "good bye? Tell her, you are going away; that you cannot keep your compact, and say "good bye too."

"I'll do anything you advise. I've nothing to lose; and even though she be angry, I'd rather see her angry than not see her at all."

Next day we rode down and surprised the whole family by our intelligence. I believe the doctor, whose brain was generally too confused to see much that was going on, thought we had both taken leave of our senses; though he altered his opinion slightly when Dick told him of the terms he had let his farm upon.

Miny did not give me a chance to see how she took it, for directly Dick began to talk of leaving the colony she disappeared. And as the afternoon was wearing away without her appearing again, I went off in search of her, determined, if possible, to say a word in my friend's behalf. I found her in the garden. She had evidently been crying, and was still too much agitated to trust herself to speak. So when I joined her, she merely looked up, then went on with some work she held.

"Miny," I said, rushing at once at the difficulty, "I have come to look for you. I wanted to speak to you alone. You know what old friends we are."

"I'm not likely to forget it. Whatever you came to say, please say quickly. I am ill and nervous to-day, and cannot promise to be patient."

"Has your father——?" I began, but she stopped me hastily.

"Please say what you came to say."

"Well, then, Miny, you know how Dick Hyde loves you, and you know why he is going away. Can you not give him a single thread of hope?"

She looked up in my face——not a hasty glance, but with a long searching gaze. I could almost feel her eyes probing my inmost thoughts. At first they were hard and reproachful; but gradually a softer expression somewhat of sorrow stole over them, and tears began to gather, then rolled over, and she turned away her face with a low deep sob.

"Miny, dear Miny," I said, "he loves you, and deserves your love. I do not ask you to stop him now; let him go and try what change and absence can do; but, dear Miny, give him something to hope."

"*You* wish it, Martin?"

"I do, Miny—I do from my soul. I think—nay, I am sure—you will be happier as his wife."

"Even if I do not love him—"

"He knows everything, Miny. And think, would one man in a thousand still ask you to be his wife, and be content with such love?"

"Martin!" she exclaimed, passionately.

"Forgive me, Miny. Would to heaven I could ask you to be my wife. You feel partly what I do, and that it is impossible. If you were my wife, Miny, you would not be happy."

"No, Martin, but I cannot marry another."

"Not now, but in time, dear; even if it were—"

"Hush, hush! Let time take its course, do; and say what you like; you know best, and I can trust you. But leave me for a time; I cannot see Mr. Hyde now, tell him."

"To-morrow, Miny, see him. I pledge my word his parting shall be only that of a friend."

"Well, Martin, I said I would go by your word."

"And now I shall say farewell, Miny. I shall see you in a month, or, at most, six weeks; and then, perhaps, you will let me write to Dick."

She shook her head, saying—

"How long six weeks must seem to you! There are fifty-two weeks in the year; it is well nigh six years since you left Slyndhurst; and I've been trying all these three hundred and twelve weeks to learn the very lesson you bid me learn in four, or, at most, six. Ah! Martin, men must be very different from women."

"I loved my wife, Miny."

She looked at me, then burst into tears.

"Oh! I know it, Martin. You are doing all that is right. I am weak to speak thus, when, if I could be your wife to-morrow, I should turn away. God bless you! friend and brother, I'll do all you ask me. And may I have strength to do what I ought in God's sight. Go away now, Martin. Send Mr. Hyde to-morrow, and then in six weeks he shall hear his answer.

CHAPTER XVI.

GOOD YET SAD NEWS FROM HOME.

Dick rode down next day and came back in a state of such sentimental happiness, that I was half inclined to regret the course I had taken.

"I think I shall not remain long at the diggings, Martin," he said, in a mysterious way.

"Why?"

"Well, to tell you the truth Miny has—but what an ass I am. You are at the bottom of it all. By Jove, if you were a different sort of fellow, or anything else but exactly what you are, I should feel inclined to blow your brains out, and cut my own throat afterwards. But seriously, Martin, Miny is to give me her final answer in two months. Think of that! I shall just have time to run through the country and see what's what; then down to San Francisco to wait for the mail, and hear my fate. If it's death, by Jove, there'll be a pretty row in the county paper of Lancashire; if it's life, then hey! for New Zealand and happiness."

"I shall ride down for the mail, Tobin," said Dick, the day after we had bid farewell to Miny.

"Not without calling on the doctor, eh?"

"Yes, without calling on the doctor,

friend," he replied, gravely. "I am content with my probation. I shall cross to Sydney with the return mail, and wait there for a chance to California; or, if I cannot do better, to some of the other ports, and make my way out the best way I can."

"Well, I don't mind going to town with you. I must try and get a revolver before trusting myself among the Maoris these bad times."

Accordingly we rode together. The mail was just in. So pocketing our letters, we finished our business, and started homewards, speculating upon the news we might expect. My letters were generally few and far between; but this mail brought me a bundle of newspapers and two letters, one in Trevor's writing, the other two from the firm who had all along transacted my business and that of my father and mother.

When one is far away from the old country, and separated by distance and consequently time, from those with whom our earliest interests have been joined, there is something beyond mere ordinary pleasure in receiving a letter. One looks at the superscription with an involuntary awe, knowing perhaps by personal experience that the hand that traced the well-known characters may long ere this be cold and lifeless.

Dick had lost a beloved sister since his sojourn in the colony and by some strange miscarriage of the letters received one from herself a month after he heard of her death; so that the poor fellow seemed to look upon letters with a mysterious awe, longing yet dreading to break the seal.

I opened Trevor's letter first, and glancing at the date, began to read. The first page contained a description of his arrival in

England; then followed some sentences that made my breath come quick, and the letters dance madly. With a violent effort I read on, but without understanding. Again and again I read the page, how often I know not.

"I say Martin," said Dick, with his hand on my shoulder, and half a tumbler of brandy at my lips, drink a drop, old boy. Good news wants support sometimes as well as bad."

"What is it, Dick? I cannot make it out."

"Come out into the sunshine, and I'll tell you."

I followed, carrying Trevor's half read letter in my hand. Dick had his full of newspapers.

"What is it, Dick? Am I ill, or——"

"Well! it's enough to confound a stronger

head than yours is at present. You thought your father was dead, didn't you?"

I nodded; and began to think I'd just read something about my father.

"Yes, of course you did, but you were wrong. By Jove, I'm a bad story-teller, old boy. But it does seem strange that the man you took so to, and fell in with, and all that, out here, should turn out to be your own father."

The light was dawning now. Word for word I went over the letter I held, Dick talking all the while, and then I began to understand the truth, a truth, which must have been long apparent to the reader, but hidden from those acting it—that Trevor was my father. And yet the first gladness of finding a father in such a man was but a brief blessing. The excitement of his trial and acquittal had brought on one of the heart attacks I had seen him suffering from; and the day after his name was sent forth to the world with every stigma cleared away, he was beyond shame, pain, or anxiety. The last words he had written were those added at the close of my letter, as a sort of postscript.

"If I had not seen you, my boy," he wrote, "I should never have cared to do what I have just done, but you deserve an unblemished name, and God has been merciful in giving me time."

The end must have been near when he wrote those words. For the servant whom he sent for a doctor was ordered to post the letter, and saw his hand shaking violently as he sealed it, and his last words were—

"My letter has gone to comfort Martin."

* * * *

My course was now plain, namely, to return to England, settle all that my father's sudden death had prevented him seeing to, and carry out, as far as lay in my power, his wishes.

I had a strong desire to become acquainted with some of my relatives. And no doubt all would be glad enough to know something of me, I being, in right of my father, head of the eldest branch of an ancient family.

So "home to old England," was now my cry, though with the fixed intention of returning at no distant period.

And thus after six years spent in my adopted country, during which I had seen her pass through the ordeal of civilization, I was again on my way to England, to begin a new life—a life in which the years passed on the bright shores of New Zealand, clouded as they were with the one never-fading grief and loss, shine as a green spot in a boundless desert.

Of Tom I must add one word. The poor fellow made his escape and got down to Auckland, where, after some months of incredible suffering, he died. Of Kauri, or Black, I heard no more, though the effects of his presence have been widely felt.

And now, gentle reader, farewell, and one gentle word at parting: if you are weary of the badly paid toil and slow returns of English farmiug, gather your means together, and ship your family off to New Zealand. There the honest, industrious, and sober man must succeed.

There's no grinding down the face of the poor out there; as, for one thing, there are no poor, and for another, wages are adequate to the value of time. The motto of New Zealand is "Onward;" and never was motto more truly carried out.

THE END.

CPSIA information can be obtained
at www.ICGtesting.com
Printed in the USA
LVHW040025180422
716440LV00005B/414

9 783752 594386